A RITUAL OF FIRE

THE FBI DRAGON CHRONICLES BOOK 1

J. L. HENDRICKS

J. A. CIPRIANO

WANT TO GET THIS FREE?

Sign up here. If you do, I'll send you my short story, *Alone in the Dark*, for free.

Visit J.A. on Facebook or on the web at JACipriano.com or visit J.L. on Facebook for all the latest updates.

ALSO BY J.L. HENDRICKS

~

The Voodoo Dolls

The Voodoo That You Do

New Orleans Magic

Hurricane of Magic

Council of Magic

~

Alpha Alien Abduction Tales Series

Worlds Revealed

Worlds Away

Worlds Collide

Worlds Explode

Worlds Entwined

A Shifter Christmas Romance Series

ALSO BY J.A. CIPRIANO

World of Ruul

Soulstone: Awakening

Soulstone: The Skeleton King

Bug Wars

Doomed Infinity Marine

The Legendary Builder

The Builder's Sword

The Builder's Greed

The Builder's Pride

Elements of Wrath Online

Ring of Promise

The Vale of Three Wolves

<u>Kingdom of Heaven</u>

The Skull Throne

Escape From Hell

<u>The Thrice Cursed Mage</u>

Cursed

Marked

Burned

Seized

Claimed

Hellbound

<u>The Half-Demon Warlock</u>

Pound of Flesh

Flesh and Blood

Blood and Treasure

The Lillim Callina Chronicles

Wardbreaker

Kill it with Magic

The Hatter is Mad

Fairy Tale

Pursuit

Hardboiled

Mind Games

Fatal Ties

Clans of Shadow

Heart of Gold

Feet of Clay

Fists of Iron

The Spellslinger Chronicles

Throne to the Wolves

Prince of Blood and Thunder

∾

<u>Found Magic</u>

May Contain Magic

The Magic Within

Magic for Hire

∾

<u>Witching on a Starship</u>

Maverick

Planet Breaker

1

ALYSON

As I walked into the living room, the actual site of the murder, I noticed a local crime scene guy puking into a bucket off in one corner. There were several more buckets around the room at the edges of the marked off scene.

Blood covered all the walls and pooled on the floor, making me think the victim had been drained dry before her blood was used… for something.

I stopped in the middle of the door after putting on my blue booties, the standard type we were issued to keep our feet from tracking in contaminants into the crime scene proper and looked around. The smell was already starting to get to me, and from the look of those buckets, I wouldn't be the first, nor the last to need them.

To be honest, the blood didn't bother me so much as the scene as a whole did. Why did they use such a large pentagram? Why was the blood painted on the walls? Why had they moved the table to that corner?

More importantly though, I wondered what the missing piece would be. The previous crime scenes had something missing, some piece of the puzzle denied to us by the killers.

In this one, part of the pentagram had been wiped away. Part of me hoped it had been done by the perpetrators and not some incompetent local. If it was a result of a forensic screw up and not a clue, I might blow a gasket. Chances were good that if it had been done by the murderer, finding out why would give me a clue as to who was doing this and why.

We needed to get this scene processed and fast. I'd already been waiting an hour, and while I'd used the time to interview a neighbor who claimed to see vampires, I was running out of patience. As I watched them shimmy around the scene, annoyance flooded through me. I was ready to walk around and see the crime scene from the different angles.

As I took a step closer and inhaled through my nose, I caught the tinge of something strange. It was faint, barely noticeable above the smell of blood and gore. Worse, that something had triggered my reflex to shift. That was the last thing I needed.

Shutting my eyes, I concentrated on my beast, on keeping her well below the surface. Once I was satisfied she wouldn't come out to play, I opened my eyes and looked across the room toward the human CSI guy mucking about next to the source of the scent.

There was no way he would smell it, and as I watched him, I began to worry it would fade away, or worse, he'd destroy it, before I could get close enough to get a better whiff.

"Hey, how much longer before you're done here?" I called out to the tech. "I need to get over there and check something." I gestured toward the spot. "My Spidey-sense is tingling."

The tech scraping some fresh blood off the ground into a tube looked up. "It will take as long as it takes. Leave us alone and we will be done faster. Keep pushing us and it will just take us longer."

Shutting my eyes for a second, I bit off my

reply. After all, someone here had to be the professional. Besides, while I respected the work the local teams did, considering they had found us one of our first clues about shifter involvement, I was getting anxious about that strange scent. That anxiety was starting to make me a bit testy.

"Alyson, just do what you can from here," my partner Vlad soothed. "Leave the poor kids alone. We will find these killers. You know we will."

I glanced over at him and sighed. We had only been partnered for about six months, a very intense six months, and I would be lying if I didn't say he was a very handsome man. Not that I would ever mention it to him.

Vlad was about six feet four inches, but if you asked him, he was six feet five inches. His olive complexion complemented his dark, brown hair with a few auburn highlights, and if I didn't know any better, I would have guessed he dyed his hair. Only, being a vampire, he would never go gray, just like he would never grow old.

None of that really surprised me though, since I myself was a shifter, albeit one who was trying to hide what she was. No, what I found most intriguing about my sexy partner was his scent.

He smelled like Red Hots, those little cinnamon

candies. His scent drew everyone in but it affected women most of all. Most licked their lips hungrily when they got close enough to smell him. Shoot, I did a few times when until I got used to it.

Still, the vampire was a good partner if only because when I was impatient, he was calm and collected.

I hated to say it, but I relied on his calming presence more often than I should because he knew who and what I really was. I could be myself in front of him and in return he got a trustworthy partner to watch over him during the day. That, among many things, was why we were such great partners. It was rather refreshing.

"Fine," I muttered, pointing toward the smeared break in the pentagram. "They removed something from this scene as well." The more I looked at it, the more I was certain the killers were responsible for the defacement. "My guess is that there was either something sitting in that spot or they used an uncommon symbol when they created the pentagram and wiped it. What do you think?"

Vlad's eyesight was just as good as mine but he could sometimes see things I missed. It was one more reason we worked so well together.

"Yes, I think they had a stand or something on

that spot. If they were wiping away a symbol, it would look more like a smear. This looks like something was dragged through the blood. I see jagged lines along the borders of the smear instead of straight marks." He pointed to the far edge of the area in question.

"You're right." Now that he pointed it out, I could see it clearly. "We know they had a stand or box at one of the other scenes. There, it must have picked up and left that rectangular clean spot in the middle of their ritual area. This time, they weren't as careful. My gut instinct is that it's a stand or something larger than a box, something awkward enough a lazy perp might want to drag it instead of picking it up properly."

While Vlad chewed over his thoughts, I decided to give the room another good sniff. Maybe now that I was calmer, I could identify the strange scent.

Even though Vlad had recently fed, a sufficiently bloody crime scene would make it almost impossible for him to focus. Worse, I'd seen him dab his lip with the little bottle of menthol he often used when the scent of blood was too overwhelming. In most cases, the menthol would overwhelm the bloody smell. The fact that he hadn't entered the room and had already dabbed his upper lip twice meant it was down to me to get this one.

Shifting my focus back to the scene I inhaled. This time, I started to pick out other scents. I smelled sulfur, which wasn't all that uncommon in a magical ritual of this caliber. There was something else though. Wolfsbane? Yes, definitely. Some ginger root for sure. Those were all among the usual ingredients when casting a spell, but there was one scent which has me puzzled. It couldn't be what I suspected, but if it was, I understood why my instincts went haywire.

It was still too indistinct from where we were at the edge of the ritual area. I needed to get closer to the smeared spot. The scent was starting to dissipate and if I didn't get to it soon, I would never figure it out.

"Distract the kids. I need to get closer," I whispered to Vlad so softly only he would be able to hear it.

"Why?" Vlad replied with equal softness. "Let them collect their evidence, it will only help us in the end. You can wait a little bit longer."

"Actually, I can't. A scent is evaporating. If I don't get closer, I could lose it. So, just create a distraction so I can get a bit closer and see if it's what I suspect."

"Alyson, don't cause a scene. If you suspect it's something, then it is. Take a deep breath and just breathe. Close your eyes and let me know what you sense." Vlad could be so infuriating at times, so calm and collected.

"Don't you think I already tried that? I just need to get a little bit closer to the smeared spot. That's it. I've got my booties on. I can tip-toe and not step into any blood."

Impatience was something I was working on. Maybe if I lived to be a few hundred years old like Vlad, I could master it. Until then, well, impulsiveness ruled me, it was just how I was. Disregarding Vlad's advice, I stood up on my tiptoes and slowly moved through the labyrinth of the blood and empty spots on the ground. I took four steps before I was caught.

"Hey! You can't walk in here yet." The tech I spoke with earlier stood up and put his hands on his hips. "I told you guys it would take as long as it takes. Stop right where you are. Stupid feds. You think you own all of the scenes. Well, you don't! If you aren't careful, you will contaminate the scene and we won't be able to help you."

His evil eye didn't scare me. The boy was just a young human. Too bad I couldn't shift. My full-blown dragon senses could pick up the trail of the herb easier than my human ones.

"Tim? Is that your name?" It was, of course, as I could see from the ID hanging off of his jacket pocket.

"Yes, and I'm in charge of the scene until I am finished. Get off of my evidence!" The boy was in a mood for sure.

Fortunately, those four steps and the extra moments arguing were enough to let me get a proper whiff, enough to confirm my suspicions. "Fine, fine," I relented. "I have what I need anyway."

I carefully made my way back to where I had been standing before I violated the poor tech's scene. Since this was the eleventh crime scene, I doubted he would find anything we hadn't already seen. My evidence, on the other hand, was new. What I picked up via scent wasn't something his mass spectrometer would identify.

"What were you thinking? Oh wait, you weren't." Vlad scowled as he led me out of the house.

"You'll be happy I didn't listen when you hear

what I discovered." My Cheshire Cat smile was from ear to ear. I could be a bit overly dramatic when I was right.

"Well, what did you find that was so important you had to possibly ruin uncollected evidence?" He narrowed his eyes, a stunt that never intimidated me as he hoped.

I licked my lips and looked around to make sure no one was watching or eavesdropping. It was all clear in the victim's front yard. "It was asphodel."

"Asphodel? Like the component in a death spell? The black magic component? Are you certain?" Even though Vlad didn't need to breathe, he took in a deep breath and rubbed his face.

"Yes, they were performing black magic. We've both suspected it since the start of this case, but this proves it. There are no uses of asphodel outside of the black arts. It's only used in a handful of death spells, one of which is so heinous, the magical community will kill you on the spot for performing it."

"The Death Drought hasn't been used for centuries," Vlad assured me. "I was told the spell has been lost. No one today can perform it."

Vlad knew a lot of witches, including some very powerful ones. If they told him the knowledge had been lost, they were either right or very good liars. Well, there was a third option. If this was the spell being used, it might have been recently recovered, unknown to the general witch community. After all, none of the paranormals that could use magic lived for more than a hundred years. Well, dragons could, but I was the last, so that was irrelevant unless I was going to arrest myself.

"I think it's time you paid a visit to your witchy friends." I raised an eyebrow and waited for his response.

"Alyson, be nice. They can be a little … strange, but overall, they are very nice. They have even helped me with my cases over the years."

"You know I've never been a big fan of witches." While I didn't know for sure who had killed my family, all the signs pointed toward witches. Worse, a powerful enough witch would be able to tell exactly what kind of shifter I was, and when you were trying to keep a secret like mine, well, let's just say, that double-whammy made me want to avoid them like the plague.

That said, I was a professional, or as professional as a member of a branch of the FBI that didn't technically exist could be. If the witches could help, we should visit them.

"I am aware of your dislike for them." He swept his gaze over my face like he was trying to find understanding in my features. "That is why you wanting to see them is… curious."

"Look, if you vouch for these particular witches, they have to be half-way decent." I gestured at the scene. "We need to stop this from happening again, so let's ask them for their expertise."

"**B**efore we leave, I want to call this in to command," I said as we walked to the car. "I think they need to be aware of the dangers. I doubt they have ever come up against dark magic like this before." He shrugged. "That's why they have us, after all."

Part of me didn't see the point of the phone call, other than it was protocol. Still while we had the ability to go above and beyond the rules that constrained normal FBI agents thanks to our status as "didn't technically exist," it was often better to play by the rules. It made it easier to ask for forgiveness later.

I was hoping I might find out something useful, but previous experience made me think it would be pointless. I had spent a considerable amount of time looking over past case files dealing with the paranormal. Most of them are unsolved. In fact, cold case investigations were how I started with the FBI.

Let me just say that when you're a vampire and you decide to play by the rules and grow a conscious, well, that opens a lot of doors for you.

"Fine, how about I drive while you phone in an update?" Alyson looked over at me and batted her eyes in a way that would have made my heart beat if it was still alive.

Alyson was truly beautiful, and I often thought she didn't even realize how attractive she was. Her brown hair was lustrous with red and gold highlights, a feature she showed off with her height. At just over six feet, she was quite tall for a woman. Combined with long, luscious black lashes and a natural beauty that didn't need a dollop of make-up, and you might begin to understand my attraction.

That wasn't all. She had the most intoxicating scent I've ever come across, something I especially appreciate as a vampire, and that's saying a lot with my many years and breadth of experience. Her natural scent reminded me of a winter wonderland. It was a cross between a wintergreen aroma mixed with snow and the smell of freshness in the open air.

Many of those qualities came from what Alyson was, something that very few people knew. Only a handful at the Bureau knew she was a shifter, and even less knew she was the rarest of shifters, a dragon. If she shifted, you were in serious trouble, and not just because of the power that a dragon had.

No, it was because dragons were supposed to be extinct, and because of that, no one could know what she really was. Keeping her secret was important not only to her, but to the Bureau and to me. After all, if someone found out, the hunters would descend on her en masse.

To help keep her secret, her file was altered to say she was a saber-toothed tiger shifter. As no one wanted to see one of those shift, considering the bloody mess that usually followed, no one questioned her when she refused to shift in front of them.

Still, none of that meant she was a decent driver since she was easily distracted. I tried to drive whenever possible, but she made a good point. Time could be of the essence now that death magic was involved.

"Just be careful and pay attention to the other drivers, please." I handed her the keys. "I mean it." I stared at her for a long moment. "This is your one shot at this."

"Vlad, just because I almost hit a curb once doesn't mean I'm a bad driver." She put her hands on her hips. "And it was your fault if you remember correctly."

I hated when she brought up the one time I lost control around her. It hadn't really been fair since we'd both been shot a few times trying to take out a house full of machinegun-toting gremlins, and I needed blood to heal.

"You were bleeding, and I was hurt," I pointed out. "How else was I to react? I told you, let me drink from you once and my desire for you will dissipate. It doesn't hurt, I promise." I gave her a wry grin. "You might even like it."

"I told you, no way, Jose. You aren't sucking my neck for any reason. I'm not going to be one of your floozies."

"If you say so." I dropped the keys into her hand. "Either way, I don't have time to indulge you now." I pulled out my phone and showed it to her. "Have to make a call. You understand."

She glowered at me as I slid into the passenger

seat, intent on ignoring her mostly because I knew it would annoy her. Ah, the small pleasures of life.

Though she didn't know it, I'd been assigned to follow her from the shadows and make sure her true identity was kept secret. With any luck, she wouldn't find out.

If she knew I'd watched her fight off a wolf shifter who had gone rogue, she'd flip her lid. He had attacked a small village of cat shifters and killed several of the elders. I'd almost stepped in to help, but she hadn't needed it. Alyson grabbed him by the snout and threw him over her shoulder before breaking his neck, all without shifting.

That was the day she earned my respect. Ever since then I had thought about her more than I probably should have. The more I saw of her strength and willingness to help others, the more attracted to her I became, an attraction that went beyond her looks or her intoxicating scent.

Once she was in the car, I pulled myself out of my memories and dialed command. It rang and rang, with no answer. Hanging up, I gave it another try to be sure, only to have the same empty ringing.

"Odd, no one is answering my call." I turned in my seat to look at Alyson. "Have you ever had your calls ignored when you were in the field?"

She scrunched up her forehead, which only made her more look desirable. "No, I don't think so. They might have let it ring a few times, but my calls have never gone unanswered. Are you sure you dialed the correct number?"

"Of course I am. It's saved to my contacts. I'll give it one last try." I did. It continued to ring with no answer, not even an answering machine or service.

"Something's not right. I think we should head back to base and make sure everything's fine." I took a deep breath even though I didn't need air and tried to calm myself. It was probably nothing, but with death magic, one could never be too careful. After all, whoever was pulling these crimes had to know the FBI would eventually be involved. Maybe they were mopping up loose ends.

"I wouldn't worry. They have a squad of wolf shifters and vampires who are always onsite. It should be just fine." Alyson was always very confident in our security forces back at base. She was probably right but still …

"Turn right at the next light. It will get us back onto the freeway."

"I do know how to get back. You can relax. Everything's fi…"

Before she could finish her sentence, something slammed into our car, throwing us into a sideways skid as an explosion of heat and sound blew the trunk open. The shriek of metal filled my ears as the car lurched up onto its front wheels, bumper skidding across the street as gravity fought against the force of the explosion.

"Hold on!" Alyson cried, bracing herself against the steering wheel as we slammed back down on the ground.

The shock of the impact ripped through me as Alyson stomped on the gas, sending us lurching forward in a spray of sparks and smoke. She turned the steering wheel from the left to the right in long arcs, trying to use the front wheel drive to our advantage and keep us from going into a deadly tumble as another explosion slammed into the asphalt to our right.

The vehicle went into a skid as the force of the explosion practically spun us around. The smell of burning tar filled my nose moments before the airbags deployed. The sound of it nearly shattered my too-sensitive hearing as the cushion slammed me backward into the seat.

"Flames and cauldrons!" Alyson cursed, tearing the airbag free with a swipe of her arm as she tried to maneuver us away. Another explosion rocked through the vehicle, and as Alyson tried to turn away from it while engaging the gas, another explosive slammed into us, flipping us over onto the driver's side while we careened down the highway, scraping along the asphalt in a shower of sparks.

To make matters worse, fire was making its way inside of the vehicle through the back seat from whatever had hit our trunk. Damn.

We needed to get out of here now. Or at least, I did. Alyson was fireproof, even in her human form, one of the many benefits of being a dragon shifter. Unfortunately, vampires were extra susceptible to fire. If I was caught in the flames, I wouldn't even have time to blink before it was all over.

"Alyson, the car is on fire," I cried right before the sound of metal digging into stone filled my ears. I swung my head around and saw Alyson's face was contorted in effort. She'd thrust her left arm out through the shattered window and into the asphalt itself. Her hand had shifted into a dragon's claw, those razor-sharp talons dragging along the pavement and slowing us down.

"Almost…there." Alyson's brow knit in grim determination as she dug in deeper, scales shifting up her forearm but stopping before the elbow..

I had never seen her partially shifted. Didn't even realize she could do something like that. The control she must have had was crazy. Still, I knew she wouldn't be able to stop us in time for it to matter, and while she was fireproof, I doubted she was explosion proof too. If this car went up, she might not make it.

That wasn't something I was okay with. "Alyson, shift and get out. You can survive if you shift."

"No," she insisted through gritted teeth. "We both make it out alive."

The car was slowing down as she continued to tear up the blacktop, even as the flames started to consume the back seats. Metal tore away from the frame on Alyson's side and for a moment, I was certain that this was it, that the rest of the door would tear free and pull Alyson under the vehicle with it. To my surprise, though, all of a sudden, we jerked to a stop as the front end crashed into something.

3
_____

VLAD

"What? What did we hit?" I put my hand to my head and pulled it away with something sticky. Blood was flowing down the side of my face. This wasn't good, especially if the car was still on fire.

I whirled around and saw flames were no longer climbing over the back of the car. In fact, most of the back of the car was gone. Good, that'd buy us time to get out.

As blood trickled into my eyes from a cut on my forehead, I quickly surveyed the scene. Somehow, the airbag that should have saved me was a mass of torn fabric, and there was a dent in the dash. I must have hit my head when we crashed into whatever had stopped us.

"We hit a telephone pole, which was good

because not only did it stop us, it tore away the flaming half of the car." Alyson looked at me as I hung in the seatbelt above her. Like mine, her airbag was also a torn-up mess. Her hand had already shifted back to smooth human flesh. "Are you all right? You're bleeding."

"Yeah, I'm fine." It wasn't even much of a lie. I wasn't feeling any pain, too much adrenaline was flooding through my system. "What about you?"

"I'm sore but fine. Let me get up before you release your belt buckle. I don't need you falling on top of me in here." She unbuckled her seatbelt and stood on shaky legs. "We need to get you out of here. Dawn is nearing, and we're still a long way from base."

She sucked in a couple raspy breaths, making me wonder how hurt she was. It was hard to tell with a shifter so powerful. If I had tried what she had, well, I don't think I would have had an arm afterward.

"Okay, just tell me what you want me to do, Alyson," I said, reaching for my seatbelt. Part of me was surprised it was strong enough to keep me suspended.

"Slowly release your belt, and I'll help you keep your head upright." She put her hands on my shoulder in an effort to hold me up as I unbuckled the seatbelt to escape from the death trap. "How did anyone know we were going back to base? Were we just in the wrong place at the wrong time?"

Alyson breathed heavily as I let my legs fall to the side of the car and stood up straight. "I don't know what just happened. All I know is someone attacked us with either a small rocket or missile or something. That first explosion was pretty large. The others though, they weren't as big. Speaking of which, I can smell gas." I inhaled again, and this time, I nearly panicked. "And smoke. I think there's still fire under the car. We need to get out of this metal box before it explodes." Fear surging through my veins, I kicked out the front windshield and scrambled through.

"Right behind you." Alyson was close on my heels. While she wouldn't burn, if the gas tank exploded, the shrapnel could be deadly.

"There." I pointed to a stand of trees just a few hundred feet away. "Let's go."."

We both ran, well, quickly hobbled to the trees as the car exploded. Immense heat rolled our way, flinging scattered pieces of steel, glass, and plastic in every direction. I braced myself, throwing one arm up as I tried to keep the shockwave from flinging me from my feet. If I'd been human, I'd have landed on my butt, but us vampires, well, we're a bit tougher. Even still, the force made my gut swim, and if it hadn't been for Alyson bracing herself against me, I'd have probably landed on my back anyway.

As I stared at the remnants of the car, and watched the pre-dawn sky light up like the Fourth of July with all of the metal raining down and bits of fire billowing out, I couldn't help but think we were lucky. If we'd been normal agents, we'd have been dead four times over.

"Do you see anyone?" Alyson asked. Although still better than a human's, in her human form, her vision wasn't quite as good as mine.

She had been holding me up against the tree and her question made me realize how close we were. The smell of her blood, combined with my injuries started to trigger the primal, dark side of me, and before I knew what was happening, my fangs began to elongate.

"Alyson, I think I've lost more blood than I can handle right now." I licked my lips as she stared at my fangs. I knew part of it was the injuries, but part of it had been the crime scene, the sudden rush of adrenaline, and now the closeness of her special blend of blood. All of it was nearly too much.

"Flames and cauldrons." Alyson cursed, stepping back from me and running her hand over her face. "You do have a large gash on your head, and while head wounds bleed a lot, you shouldn't have lost enough to need to feed." Her jaw set as she looked at me, thoughts swimming through her eyes. "How much of my blood do you need to heal?"

She took a shuddering breath as she waited for my answer. I couldn't look her in the eye, no matter how hard I tried. My eyes stayed focused on the ground in front of her.

"Look, I know you don't want to give me any." I shut my eyes, summoning every bit of willpower I had. "Let's just find a place to hide from the sun."

"That doesn't answer my question." She reached under her suit jacket, pulled out a metal flask, and offered it to me. "Will this be enough?"

"You brought blood?" I asked, confused.

"I've thought about the perils of partnering with a vampire." Her eyes flicked from me to the flask and back again. "And I don't want you drinking from me. Not now, not ever." She grimaced.

"Alyson…"

"Just take a small amount, enough to get you through the day. Hurry, we still have to find you shelter before the sunrise or before whoever attacked us comes looking to make sure we died in the explosion." She shoved the flask into my hands.

"Thank you." I opened the flask and took a whiff. It smelled fresh, and while it wasn't hers, I could tell it was human. Interesting. "Where did you get it?"

"Where do you think?" She raised an eyebrow at me. "I requested it." She shrugged.

"Oh." I wasn't quite sure what I'd expected honestly, but somehow the thought that she'd gotten it through "official" channels irked me. It made me wonder what reasoning she'd given.

Still, as I turned my gaze back to the flask, I couldn't really get mad at her. The blood called to me, and as much as I hated to say it, I could smell her scent on the flask.

Shutting my eyes for a brief moment, I upended the flask and gulped down the blood.

"Are you all right?" she asked as I licked my lips clean. "Was it enough?"

"Yes." I suppressed the part of me that wanted to smirk and focused on the thoughtful smile the better half of me wished to show. "Thanks for thinking of me."

"You're welcome." She breathed deeply for a moment before clapping me on the shoulder. "Now let's go."

I tried to catch her eyes, but she avoided my gaze. She was most likely embarrassed. Not wanting her to feel embarrassed over my enjoyment of the blood, I kept it professional.

"I appreciate what you did, Alyson." I smiled as best I could even though I was more embarrassed with myself. My partner was carrying around a flask of blood because she was worried she'd have to let me drink from her in a tight spot. Man, what did that say about me? "Thank you."

"You're welcome," she said, voice a bit clipped, a bit strained.

"You know, you're really amazing," I added, gesturing down at myself even though she wasn't looking at me. "I'm already starting to feel my injuries heal." I touched my forehead, noting how the gash was already stitching itself back together. I'd be back to normal in no time.

Either way, as she turned to me and gave me a small smile, I knew one thing to be certain. Alyson made me feel alive.

4

ALYSON

The way Vlad looked at me made me uncomfortable in a way I didn't like to admit. I was too busy to have many boyfriends over the years, plus secret identity and all. So, I never imagined I would be so turned on by a vampire. It was not something I was proud of. Vlad was hot, sure. I'd give him that much but the way he looked at me, oh man. I was in trouble.

"Vlad, we need to find you some shelter and fast." I took another breath, trying to push away the sudden influx of untoward thoughts. It was not going well. Still, even if I was the kind of girl who could ignore the whole blood drinking thing, fawning over him now wouldn't get him to safety before the sun came up. No. Now was the time to focus.

"Thank you. I know helping me in such a way is not a requirement of the job nor is it something you ever wanted to do. Please know how grateful I am." Vlad bowed his head in thanks to me.

"You're welcome."

What else could I say to a vampire who had thanked me for giving him a flask full of blood? The worst part was I couldn't even be mad at him for needing blood right now since it wasn't his fault. He had fed before coming to work, which should have been more than enough. How was he to know we were going to be blown up?

All of these crime scenes and not once had anything happened to us. All I could think about was the asphodel. The perps must have realized they had left a trace of it behind and now they wanted to clean up after themselves. That clean-up included us.

"We've got to get going, Vlad. Now." We had at best an hour before the sun came up, and despite his quirks, I didn't want to watch my partner and friend die today.

"I don't sense anyone near. Do you know this area? Are there any houses or offices close by?" His words made me smile. While it seemed like Vlad had been everywhere, the high desert outside of Los

Angeles was one of those rare places he hadn't visited.

"We are in between Palmdale and Santa Clarita," I explained. "There will be some abandoned buildings along the highway if we want to try and travel parallel to route 14. I don't recommend it though. Whoever is after us will be watching the highway."

I knew of a few places off the beaten path that might be better. They weren't the type of places vampires frequented or FBI agents for that matter, not unless we were arresting people. That very fact gave us the best chance of escape and survival.

Vlad scanned our surroundings, no doubt trying to see if he could sense anyone, friend or foe, nearby. "What do you suggest?"

"I know of a place. It's dangerous but close enough we might be able to make it in time. They hate outsiders, and I may have arrested a couple of their crew a few years back. So, I doubt they will be very welcoming." I shrugged. "But honestly, I'll take my chances with a few human criminals who may or may not remember me over letting you burn."

"Of course, that also means they will be hostile to anyone searching for us." Vlad nodded, and I had to agree, there was a small silver lining. "And I agree. Not burning would definitely be optimal." He looked at me then. "Will you be safe while I sleep?"

Vlad's words made me bristle. He was always trying to protect me. What he needed to remember was I could easily take out an entire building if I shifted and used my dragon fire.

"I'll be fine—"

"Why don't you shift and take us somewhere else, safer?" Vlad gave me a hopeful look.

"Vlad, you know why I can't do that. If someone sees me flying, my secret would be out, and my life will be over. It's a last resort option. If we don't get to shelter in time, I will shift and fly us to Vasquez Rocks. There are a few caves we can hide out in while you sleep the day away, but until that happens, we're going to hoof it."

Even if no one saw us, hiding in a tourist destination was far from ideal. You never knew when a large tour group would show up. The last thing we needed was someone trying to force us out of a cave during the light of day or worse, trying to wake up a vampire before sunset.

"Come on. If we jog we'll probably make it in about a half-hour. Follow me." I began a light pace as I got my bearings.

While I didn't have anything broken, my legs hurt and the arm I had used to stop the car was sore. Both of us had been beaten up pretty good from the crash and the explosion.

It took us a bit more than thirty minutes to arrive at our destination. It was a shoddy looking bar, a real dive, way off the highway. In fact, a good part of the way we had been going along a dirt road instead of pavement. Since it was so early in the morning, the place was closed. From my investigation before, I knew they always left a side door unlocked in case one of their crew needed to get in. No need to keep it locked tight when everyone knew a biker gang owned the place.

"Wait. You want to hide out inside of a biker bar? Are you crazy? Even if they leave me alone to sleep, you will be seen as a target. It's too dangerous." Vlad's caution over the idea was why I hadn't told him where we were headed. Better to ask for forgiveness than permission after all.

"These guys aren't so bad. After we busted them for illegal weapons, their club president decided they needed to switch gears. Most of them actually have real jobs now. The place will be empty for the majority of the day. Trust me."

I walked over to the side door. When I pulled on it, it was locked. "Strange."

I figured I might as well knock. I hadn't been lying when I told Vlad these guys had mostly gone legit.

To my surprise, a woman I didn't recognize opened the door. "Can I help you?"

I put on my best, most persuasive smile. "Yes, we were in a car accident a few miles back. Your bar is the first place we've come to. Can we come in? Maybe call someone to come and get us? For some reason, my phone isn't working."

Her eyes narrowed. "Sorry, we're closed." She moved to shut the door in my face.

"Please." Vlad took over, flashing his million-watt smile, and I swear the woman melted. "We're hungry and tired. My friend hurt her leg in the accident. We just need a place to stay while we wait for a ride. I promise we won't be any trouble."

"Of course. You must be so tired and thirsty. Please come in." The woman ignored me entirely and, heck, she almost closed the door on me. All her attention was focused on Vlad the entire time.

Vampires had a way with human women. I have never seen one turn him down for anything. While it annoyed me at times, it could also be helpful.

Vlad never took his eyes off the woman as he asked her, "Could you please help me and my friend and get us some water? Alyson? Do you want anything else?"

"Yes, I'm hungry," I nodded as I looked to our new host. "Do you have anything to eat?"

She completely ignored me and continued to stare into Vlad's eyes. "I'm Patricia. What's your name?" She actually flung her blonde hair over her shoulder. The woman wasn't very tall, but she was kind of pretty in a skanky way. I didn't realize daisy dukes were still in fashion complimented by her barely-there tank top that left nothing to the imagination.

"I am Vlad, and this is my friend, Alyson." He gestured to me but she continued to stare longingly at my partner.

"Hi, Patricia?" I resisted the urge to wave my hand in front of her face or snap my fingers in her ear. "I could use some water and anything you have to eat. If it's any trouble, we can pay." I really was hungry and thirsty. Getting blown up really does take a lot out of a person, even a paranormal one.

"There are some peanuts on the bar. A fridge underneath has some cold water bottles, help yourself." Her tone was distracted, almost dismissive, as she took Vlad's hand and led him to a booth in a corner.

I tried my best not to listen to their conversation while I searched the bar for the water and anything they had to eat besides peanuts. Under the bar was the mini-fridge Patricia had mentioned and in that, I found the water bottles. I drained one bottle immediately before grabbing another.

The run must have dehydrated me more than I realized. I was fireproof, not fatigue proof. I was still thirsty and plenty hungry. Now that we were inside, and Vlad had done his vampire thing on our host, I was a lot less concerned about him, and a lot more concerned about myself. After all, I'd have to stay here while he slept.

Worse, after all the effort, I was starving. All I could think about was a ham and cheese omelet with bacon and hash browns. I wondered if they had a kitchen. I wasn't above making my own meal while the chick flirted with my partner.

I could hear them both laughing and talking about her. Vlad was good at making women feel comfortable, even in awkward situations. However, it was time for him to sleep. We were cutting it close as it was.

I walked over to their table and handed Vlad a

water bottle. He didn't really drink water, but we had to keep up appearances. "Hey, how are you feeling? You were pretty shaken up by that crash. Maybe you should lie down and get some rest?"

"Yeah, I probably should. Patricia, do you have a room I could sleep in for a little while?" Vlad smiled at the woman who was under his thrall. "It must be dark as I have a medical condition that makes me very sensitive to sunlight."

"Of course. I could keep you company, if you like." She actually fluttered her eyelashes at him.

Vlad licked his lips and looked between me and Patricia. "Thank you for the offer, but something tells me I wouldn't be able to sleep with a woman like you in the room with me."

She tried to act coy by looking down and putting a hand over her mouth, but I knew better. "Of course. You should sleep. The only quiet room without a window is the storeroom. I'm here to stock the shelves before the guys show up, so I'll grab what I need and you can sleep in there."

The annoying chick left and came back with a pillow and blanket for Vlad. "Sorry I don't have anything better, but the floor isn't too bad." She shrugged.

"This is just fine. Thank you, Patricia. Let me

know once you are done with the storeroom." Vlad smiled at the woman before she turned around.

When Patricia went back into the storeroom, I stared Vlad down. "What was that all about?"

"Alyson, don't worry. She's a means to an end, that's all. She will help us until we can get in touch with command. Should I need more blood, who would you prefer I take it from? You?"

I shook my head. Absolutely not.

"Of course not. Patricia will be more than accommodating for my … needs. This way you don't have to worry about them anymore." His smirk told me he knew how much he had affected me.

Stupid vampire! If we weren't partners, I might have considered a night with him. But since we were, it wasn't something I could ever do if I wanted to be able to keep working with him. That sort of complication was the last thing I needed.

On top of that, I wasn't the one-night stand kind of woman and Vlad wasn't the relationship type of man. Ignoring my attraction to him was the best thing for both of us.

Patricia returned a few minutes later. She walked Vlad to the storeroom and I followed.

"Okay, Vlad. The room is all yours. I hope you feel better."

I would need to keep an eye on him while he slept. The last thing we needed was a biker going in there and not coming out. When woken abruptly, Vlad had a tendency to attack first, and ask questions after he drank an intruder dry. He was the epitome of a hangry sleeper or maybe it was just self-preservation? Either way, it was always dangerous to wake up a vampire before they were ready.

I tried to linger behind as Patricia turned toward the main bar to leave, but she gave me the evil eye. "Excuse me, you can just wait in the bar. There is only room for one person to sleep in here." The jealous vibe she gave off was obvious but if she thought I wanted to sleep with Vlad, she had another thing coming.

"Don't worry, I'm just looking for the ladies' room and maybe a kitchen? Is there somewhere I can make some breakfast for myself?"

I tried to act like I was just giving myself the nickel tour. I looked into all the open doors as we passed them on the way to the front. This place was really empty. I'm surprised they left Patricia here all alone. Maybe they figured no one would mess with a biker chick?

"Down the hall to your left is the ladies room," she said, pointing to help indicate her directions. "Keep going and on your right, you'll find the kitchen. Since you're making breakfast, you might as well make enough for me as well. After all, I am letting you hang around until your help arrives. Hey, have you called anyone for help yet?"

"I was going to wait until you finished helping Vlad," I smiled as I passed her to head to the ladies' room. "I'll call my boss and see if he's up."

"Good luck," she called out before I entered the ladies room, which left me wondering why I would need luck to call my boss.

After I cleaned up a bit, I tried calling the office. No answer, just like what had happened to Vlad when he tried before. Something was really off. The FBI operated twenty-four hours a day, seven days a week. The office never closed. I had heard that even during the Northridge Earthquake, they had forwarded the phones to another location so someone was answering them.

Sure, I could call the Washington DC branch but they were all humans. None of them knew what was up, as far as I knew, and I was fairly sure my boss wouldn't like random FBI guys calling him to ask who I was since I didn't technically exist.

The only one outside of the paranormal division who knew Vlad and I were on the team was the head honcho himself, Director Moss. Maybe I needed to get his direct line for emergencies like this. It made me wish I hadn't lost my satellite phone when the car exploded. That'd be able to get through even if the cellphones weren't working.

Still mulling over what to do, I tapped out an email on my phone and sent it, but after the last three hadn't been answered, I didn't have high hopes.

Sighing, I made my way to the kitchen. It was in surprisingly good shape for how much of a dive the place looked on the exterior, and sure enough, they had a commercial fridge full of delicious ingredients, including everything I needed for breakfast and more. It was a touch surprising, to be honest.

Patricia walked in as I considered our options.

"Whatcha making? It looks like you're just standing there, not working." This woman was a piece of work. If she thought she was going to bully me around, she was in for a rude awakening.

"I just tried calling my office. No one answered, not even a machine. This isn't right." I scratched my head and when I pulled my hand back, I noticed some dried blood. Great, all I needed was a head injury at this point.

"Haven't you seen the news? The phones are down all over the place."

"What? What's going on? Is that why you said good luck earlier?" I had been completely out of the loop since we started our investigation last night.

"I'll turn the TV on to the local news. Bring our breakfast out when you're done." She turned on her heels and left me alone in the kitchen with more questions than answers.

My stomach gurgled its displeasure at waiting any longer for food. "Okay, calm down. I'll feed you." Sometimes, my stomach was more beastly than I was.

I don't think I had ever cooked breakfast so fast in my life. Once I had two plates ready, I brought them into the bar. It was the least I could do since she was letting us crash here. She annoyed me, sure, but she was helping us out.

Besides, my bad mood was probably because someone tried to blow up me and my partner. I was tired and sore, but it was nothing a few hours of sleep couldn't cure. When I woke up, I would probably be in a much better mood.

Until then, I needed to remember I was an FBI agent, trained to deal with idiots and criminals.

I took a seat close to the TV screen over the bar displaying the local Channel Seven news. "Hey, can you turn that up?"

Patricia glanced over at me and turned up the volume with a nearby remote.

The anchorman paused as a picture of a bunch of downed telephone poles appeared behind him. "Earlier tonight a group claiming to be the People United Against Corporate America eco-terrorist group attacked our telecommunication infrastructure. Authorities have told us they are working on getting services back up, but it could take up to two days to get everything repaired.

"The Mayor has asked everyone to keep going about business as usual. Don't let these homegrown terrorists stop business or life. Don't try to use the phone, unless it's an emergency. Our local emergency services need any bandwidth we have. We will keep you updated as more details arrive."

I ignored the rest of the news report as it moved to other stories that weren't important to our current situation. Though this terrorist attack was a big problem, it was also something of a relief. Maybe nothing was wrong with our base, and they just couldn't receive our calls? It also explained the lack of response to my emails, and made me feel better about the satellite phone.

The FBI no doubt had their hands full with the terrorist threat and wouldn't want to deal with us right now. Worse, it meant if we went back in, there was a good chance we'd be pulled off the current case and forced to help with that.

No. We were under the radar for a reason. The best thing to do would be to continue working this case, especially since someone had tried to blow us up. Then, once we figured it out, we could go help with the terrorist thing. Besides, that wasn't really my sort of scene anyway. Not unless it was magic-related anyway.

As I let that realization settle over me, I looked around and sighed. Now, I just had to figure out how to spend the day in a biker bar.

5

ALYSON

"Whoa, who do we have here?"

I woke to find a tall, burly biker putting his arm around my shoulders. I had been sleeping in a back booth of the bar and hadn't realized it was already past two in the afternoon.

I rubbed my eyes and looked at the guy before shoving his arm off me. "I'm just passing through. The phones are down and my car's totaled."

"Was that your car I saw about five miles down the road?" The stranger's bearded face appeared to be smiling, but there was so much bush I couldn't be sure. This guy looked more like a ZZ Top reject than a biker. How could he ride with that huge beard flapping in his face? Maybe he tucked it in his shirt when he rode?

"Yup, that was ours. My friend is here too. We tried to call home but can't get the phones to work. Does yours?" There were at least some phones working, if I believed the news. Maybe ZZ Top's phone was on a different service and if I tried a different one, it was possible I might get through to command.

"Nope, phones are all down today. You're lucky you were so close to us. This is a great place to wait out the apocalypse. We are stocked with plenty of food and drink." He looked over to the bar where another burly man was watching us.

"That's right, Rhett. Whatcha want, little lady? Bourbon and Coke? Beer? Please don't tell me you want wine. We don't stock swill." The bartender laughed.

"Uh, I think I'll stick with water, thanks." I really hoped these guys would leave me alone, but a new woman in a biker bar was probably like candy to a kid, something they couldn't pass up.

"Oh, come on babe. I think you'll have more fun if you have a few drinks."

The guy next to me was just trying to get me drunk or drugged. I wasn't really sure which. Either way, I wasn't going to fall for it. Even if I did partake, little did they know that alcohol didn't affect me like most women. My system burned it off so fast, it would probably take an entire week of drinking non-stop to get drunk. Well, that might be exaggerated, but it would take a long time and a ton of booze, more time and booze than I'd ever give these guys.

"Sorry, I can't really party today. I need a clear head so I can find a way home, but I won't stand in your way, though. Feel free to drink. I'll just wait for my friend to feel better. The crash probably hurt him more than he's willing to admit." I needed some way to make these guys think Vlad wouldn't be an issue so they would leave him alone.

"Is he your boyfriend or something?" the bartender asked. "I don't see a ring on your finger."

"Not even close. We work together." I turned to ZZ Top and put on a polite smile. "I'm Alyson. What's your name?"

I hadn't seen these guys before so I needed real names to put with their faces in my memory banks. My brain was pretty good at sorting a face to a name. It was rare I forgot someone.

"I'm Rhett and my buddy behind the bar is Stoner." The guy next to me smiled, I think. There were some teeth in the bush covering his face, so I assumed it was a smile.

"Nice to meet you, Rhett. Stoner? I take it that's a nickname?"

Most of the guys I busted a few years ago used street names and it was a common practice with biker gangs in general. Rhett seemed like a normal name unless he was a fan of *Gone With The Wind*.

"Yup, none of us use our real names. I wanted to name him Skunk since he likes to smoke the stuff so much, but our president had another member he wanted to name skunk. It suits him better, anyway." Rhett and Stoner both busted up laughing.

I guessed it meant one of their members really stunk to high heaven.

"Rhett, where did your name come from?"

"My Momma named me Rhett after some dumb movie she loved to watch. It just kinda stuck, even when I joined the club." *Gone With The Wind.* Okay, that one was sort of cute.

The door to the place flew open and a group of eleven bikers walked in. Some had women with them.

Rhett stood up and pointed to me. "Guys, look what we got here! A fresh recruit."

"No, I'm not a recruit. Just trying to wait out the phone issue so I can call for a ride home. That's all." I took a deep breath as my inner dragon sensed their threat in the air and tried to push her down. Now wasn't the time to get angry. Not with Vlad still asleep. "Not interested in becoming part of your club."

Motorcycle clubs were not for me. Nothing against it personally, but I just didn't like riding down the open road on a motorcycle. It always just made me miss flying.

"I don't think that's how it works. Am I right, Riot?" As he spoke, Stoner licked his lips. As I watched him envision me naked, my hands curled into fists.

Now was when I really needed my partner to help calm me down. I could deal with a dozen crazy men as long as they kept their crazy to themselves. Once it moved to more than that, well, I might not be able to keep a lid on my dragon, and once she came out to play, all bets were off.

"That's right." Riot, one of the guys who had walked in, leered at me. "Any woman who comes through these doors is fair game for the club members. Sorry, darlin'. You just became our entertainment for the day." I stood up and stared them all down. "Guys, I've had a rough night, you really don't want to mess with me. I have zero patience for stupid men who don't know when to back off. My partner and I came in here intending to pay for our food and drinks and just hang out until we could get a ride back to LA. Just leave me be and there won't be any trouble."

Of course, one of them just had to go and be an idiot. Some short guy who probably had Napoleon Syndrome or something came up and tried to pull me to him.

I pushed him back and he came at me again. This time I brought my knee right up between his legs. No matter how much I tried, I couldn't be gentle. The guy fell on the ground moaning while he grabbed his jewels.

The rest of the guys laughed.

"You got spunk." Riot stalked over to the guy on the floor and helped him up before grinning at me. "I like you. All right, you can stay as long as you pay." With that, he turned back to the little man. "Leon, how many times have I told you, don't grab women unless they want you to?" Shaking his head, Riot glanced back at me. "This happens all the time. He feels like he has to prove he's some big Casanova or something. He almost always ends up on the floor." He shrugged in a way that made me think they'd set the guy up. I wasn't sure why, but that almost annoyed me more.

Riot walked Leon to the back of the place. Hopefully, I wouldn't have to see him again. Fortunately, the rest of Riot's guys were more disciplined than the little guy and were more than happy to leave me alone after that.

I wound up taking a seat in the booth closest to the hall which led to the storeroom where Vlad was sleeping. I had at least four more hours to go before Vlad would be up. As I took my seat again, the red vinyl covered seat made a squelching noise.

It was going to be one long day.

My hand instinctively covered my mouth as I yawned. Another plus of being a dragon shifter was that I didn't need much sleep, but I did like to get at least six hours. So far, I had less than four and most of those had been interrupted by Patricia cleaning the place up.

The news kept me up to date. Telephone services were slowly coming back on throughout the valley. Now I just needed the city and high desert to get their phone services restored, something the news reporters said wouldn't happen until the next day. The inactivity and inability to act on our case was the most infuriating thing but I kept that frustration in check. Getting angry wouldn't get anything done.

The day dragged on and most of the guys left me alone, until one of them decided I needed a friend to talk to.

Sidling up to me, Riot put an unopened beer bottle in front of me. "How long is your friend going to be?" He sat down into the opposite end of the booth and popped the top off the bottle with his bare hands.

Before I could answer, I heard a door open and close. It was so soft that only I could have heard it. Vlad was awake.

"I think he's probably up now," I said, sliding out of the booth. "Thanks for letting me wait out the day." I gestured toward the window where the sun was dipping over the horizon.

"Is that so?" Riot asked, watching me move in a way that made me think he didn't believe me.

"It is so." Almost casually, Vlad walked up next to me and licked his lips. My own unexpectedly thumping heart calmed down as he glanced down at Riot.

"You missed something, right here." I pointed to a red drop on the side of his chin, and as I did, I wondered who he had fed from.

Vlad used a finger to swipe it away, looking at it for a moment before putting the finger into his mouth. Scrunching his nose at the taste, he looked around at the gang. "Word of advice. You all should eat better. Your blood doesn't taste very good. It's too fatty and full of stale alcohol."

I'd never heard him complain about his meals before and it was so shocking, I ignored Riot who was staring at my partner open-mouthed. "I didn't realize vampires preferred those who ate healthy."

"Of course we do," he explained as our host continued to stare in shock. "Just like humans prefer organic foods, vampires prefer humans who eat organic. Those pesticides used in food production taste awful. Don't even get me started on the steroids most companies use in their cattle. It makes your blood taste like sewage."

"Maybe you should be choosier about who you drink from." I crossed my arms over my chest, suddenly annoyed with him even though I wasn't sure why.

"I don't see you offering." Vlad shrugged. "Is that going to change?" When I didn't respond he nodded. "Thought not."

"Are you really talking about drinking blood?" Riot asked, voice concerned as his eyes flicked from Vlad to me and back again.

"Yes." Vlad nodded. "But don't worry, I didn't

take much from any of your friends." He gestured back at the room, and I realized several of the men were standing stock still, their eyes dazed in that "I've been mind-whammied" by a vampire way.

"You did what?" Riot asked, leaping to his feet.

"All right…" I mumbled as Riot burst past us to shake one of the men still standing there dazed. "What are you going to do about these witnesses? Erase their minds? Do you have enough juice for it?"

"I'll need to take just a little bit more from each of them. It should give me more than enough juice to erase us from their recent memories." Vlad looked at me before making his way to the first biker. "Consider it done."

"All right, I'll make sure no one leaves. Make it quick." I stood in front of the main door and watched as Vlad practically went supersonic. Well, it wasn't that fast, but he didn't spend much time taking a little sip from each of the twenty one bikers and chicks in the room.

I watched in awe as my partner then proceeded to alter their memories. He told them to forget ever seeing us and to go about their business like we weren't even there. It made the rest of the day pass quite comfortably.

"Looks like it's dark enough," Vlad said, startling me away from the news program. I hadn't even heard what was going on because I'd been too busy staring at the anchor's cheek mole. "Let's get out of here."

"We still don't have a car?" I mumbled, looking helplessly at my phone.

"Right, car." He nodded before getting to his feet. "Say, can one of you fine upstanding gentlemen lend us a car?"

"Sure thing, boss," Riot said, his eyes going glassy as he turned to look at us. "Mine's out front." He held out a pair of keys.

"We can leave it in LA somewhere," Vlad said, taking the keys and turning to offer me his free hand. "Once they report it missing, they'll get it back. No one will know we were here. Probably the best thing for all involved since we can't call in their illegal weapons possession."

Vlad was right. If the phones were working I would have called this whole situation in. We would have been picked up hours ago and been back on out investigation already. On the other hand, if the phones were working, we wouldn't have been in this situation in the first place.

6
___
VLAD

I hated removing memories. It was as though I was stripping a portion of a human's soul. Doing anything against another living being's wishes was not something I enjoyed even when they deserved it.

When I had woken up and heard they were threatening my partner, I couldn't stop my baser instincts from taking over. The only reason I stopped when I did was Alyson and the way she looked at me. I wasn't joking when I said I stopped because of her.

It wasn't because she would give me a hard time though. I just didn't want her to see me as a demon of the night, even though I am. Her respect was something I have always wanted.

I've killed in front of her in self-defense.

Drinking blood in front of her wasn't anything new either. But my slaughtering a room full of outlaws while draining them dry was something I'd never want her to see.

Sometimes my inner demons really ticked me off. I didn't need to be second guessing myself and my feelings for my partner. I needed those feelings to be platonic. It never worked when partners developed romantic ties, ever. I should know, I've done it too many times to count over the past two centuries.

After erasing the bikers' memories of us, Alyson and I walked outside to see what those animals loaned us.

"I wonder which vehicle it is," I said, glancing from the key in my hand to the parking lot. There weren't that many cars here, but there were enough that the thought of checking them all irked me.

"Just click the button," Alyson said, and as I turned to ask her what she meant, she snatched the key out of my hand and pointed it at the parking lot. "Sometimes I forget you're old." She gave me a quick smile as she clicked the remote. "Just click the remote and see what lights up."

Alyson laughed as the lights on the black SUV on the side of the building flashed in response to the remote. "See, works every time." She began heading toward it. "And we don't have to take a motorcycle. Bonus."

Personally, I would have preferred the 1969 Dodge Charger or the 2017 Infiniti QX80, but beggars can't be choosers.

"I suppose that is true," I said.

"What's the matter? Don't like SUVs?" Alyson chuckled and walked around to the driver's side of the vehicle. "Or were you hoping for one of the bikes so I'd have to hold you tight?"

"The thought had crossed my mind, but your hair would be a rat's nest after riding a hog." Even though I loved the idea of Alyson wrapping her arms around me while riding a motorcycle, it wasn't practical while on a case.

"I prefer riding in style and not drawing too much attention. Those loud motorcycles will turn heads wherever we go." Alyson made a good point as she unlocked the car and slid behind the driver's seat. "Now let's go."

I raised a finger to protest as I got into the passenger's seat. "I can drive. After the last time you drove, it might actually be better for me to do so."

She backhanded my chest and snorted. "Seriously? You're going to blame me for the car blowing up?"

"Look, all I'm saying is bad things happen when you drive." I shrugged as Alyson backed out of the parking space and pulled onto the highway heading back to town.

"You're not driving." She glanced at me instead of keeping her eyes on the road. "Anyway, I learned while you were sleeping that all of the phones are down, which is why we can't reach base. Some eco-terrorist group attacked the telecommunications lines. It's going to take a couple of days to get them back up, cell towers included."

"What? A terrorist attack?" I slumped in my chair and thought about the past twenty-four hours. "I don't like the timing of it. We need to pay a visit to the local coven and see what they think about this and the murders. I'm sure everyone is fine back at base if the phones are just down." I looked out the window as we pulled onto the road and stared at the night sky. "Besides, if there is a problem at HQ, the witches might be able to help."

Alyson's face turned hard. "Fine." She slowed down and made a U-turn in the middle of the street and drove toward the witches' lair.

I knew she had an issue with witches. She had a right to. Most of them were self-serving and never helped the paranormal community unless it served their purpose. This coven was different, or at least, they were different with me.

"Alyson, remember what I said. This coven has helped me many times. They even helped us with our first case." That particular fact was something I had kept to myself until now, knowing how she would have reacted if I had told her about it at the time.

She gave me a hard, sidelong glance at that. "That may be true, and I remember what you said last night. It doesn't mean they'll be helpful to the rest of our community. I wouldn't be surprised if they got something out of it whenever they helped you." The edge in her voice told me she didn't approve of my plan to visit the witches but she'd do it anyway.

That was fine. As long as we went, I could kill two birds with one stone. I'd been meaning to see the great witch, anyway. She was next on my list of people to question. Not that I suspected her. Quite the opposite, I wouldn't be surprised if someone in her coven had been attacked.

With that, Alyson shook her head and focused on the road which was a good thing, because up ahead the cars were completely stopped on the road.

"Now what?" she said, getting annoyed.

Cars were backed up all along our side of the road while the opposite lanes were moving freely. This must have been going on for a little while as people were milling about talking. Of course, the jam was deep enough that I couldn't see what the holdup was.

"Can you try calling command again? Maybe you can get a signal now?" I asked as I checked my own phone. The battery was just about out as Alyson dug out her own phone. I took the time while she dialed up command to hunt for a car charger. Thankfully the owner of this car had good tastes in cell phones as I found a charger that matched my phone in the center console. Not everyone had iPhones anymore.

By the time I finished, Alyson was shaking her head. "No luck. Figures. Our luck has certainly dried up on this case." Alyson leaned her forehead against the steering wheel.

"I can run up ahead and see what's going on. Why don't you just wait here in case the line moves?" I hopped out without waiting for her reply. There really wasn't much else we could do, after all.

About a mile up the road I could see the issue, downed power lines. Two consecutive poles were splayed across the road. I had a bad feeling about this.

Something was off. There hadn't been a storm while I slept, so they couldn't have been downed by lightning. No cars had crashed into it. Thinking it was fishy, I made my way to the bottom of the first pole to inspect how it fell over.

Once I was next to the pole, I smelled the air and realized it was the work of whomever has been committing the murders. The stench of death and black magic permeated the air. This had to have been done within the past few hours.

Was our perp trying to keep us up here or were they trying to keep someone else out of LA?

I took a closer look at the pole, and sure enough, the edges were smooth. It looked as though someone took a chainsaw to the wood. If I were going to down these lines, I would have pushed them over and let the wood break, as though something natural shoved them down, like wind or even a car accident. The way these looked, it was obvious they were taken down on purpose.

Just one more clue for our case full of clues with no answers.

Standing, I glanced around. Right at the front of the traffic jam was a man leaning against a black

Dodge Ram Heavy Duty pick-up truck. "Hey, why don't you with the truck come help me? You have a wench on that monster?" With the torque from his truck and a few strong men, we could move these poles out of the way and get traffic flowing again.

"Yeah, sure thing." He walked toward me as he surveyed the poles. "Are the lines dead? I have no interested in getting fried by power lines today."

"I don't see any sign of power arcing from the lines. We just need to move the poles back to the side of the road. No need to actually touch the lines. They'll move when we move the poles." Now I could touch the lines and be just fine although it would look odd if anyone noticed I was getting electrocuted and still standing.

My proactive attitude had gotten the attention of some other helpful-looking motorists. Nodding at them, I looked back to the truck driver. "If you could pull one of the poles back to the side using your truck while the rest of us move the other pole, it should help to keep the lines from causing any issues. You know, just in case the power is still flowing through them."

Everyone agreed to the idea and my little crew of volunteers got ready to move our pole as the driver hooked up the other to his truck, though I really didn't need their help. I just needed everyone to think I was a normal man, not a paranormal one.

We got the poles moved in no time and everyone went back to their vehicles. With a little time, the traffic began to move again. I waited by the side of the road for Alyson to pick me up.

"What happened?" Alyson said when I opened the door to the SUV.

I jumped in and when she took off, I told her the situation.

After I finished my little story and recounted what I had seen and smelled, she nodded. "I have to agree. It sounds like our killers are trying to keep us, or someone else, away. Not really sure yet." Alyson kept her eyes ahead, but I could tell from her serious expression she was focused on what this all meant for us.

We headed toward the great witch. I just hoped she was in the mood for uninvited visitors.

7

VLAD

"All right, just follow my lead and let me do the talking," I said. "Whatever you do, don't give them attitude. They could have information we need, Alyson."

My partner wasn't always the most diplomatic. Still, she was also usually right on in her estimation of people, unless she was pre-disposed to hate them before she even met them. Like with witches.

I couldn't really blame her for not trusting witches, especially with a secret like hers. Worse, from what she has learned about her family, witches were involved in their brutal deaths. Traces of magic were found at the scene of her parent's murder. Since she discovered that, she really hadn't trusted any witches. It hadn't helped that she has busted more than a few for messing with humans.

While her distrust was warranted, I hoped she would be able to trust my friends, since I trusted them with my life.

"Don't worry about me. I'll be on my best behavior. Scout's honor." She lifted her hand with three fingers up.

"That only means something if you were actually in the Girl Scouts." I quirked my mouth and shook my head. She was going to be a handful on this one, I could feel it.

Now, this particular coven of witches lived in an old industrial complex, from factories to management offices. Every building was all set up with a vast array of magical booby traps for anyone who was stupid enough to break-in. I'd seen one man go up in flames when he tried to enter without permission. If you had any idea of what witches could do, you would be stupid to mess with them.

While the older buildings looked like they were about to fall apart, most of their decrepitude a glamour woven by the witches to keep people away, the main business office was in great shape. It doubled as a storefront for their business where the coven sold soy candles, all-natural body soaps, and shampoos, the type of products yuppies and hippies alike spent their hard earned money on, under the company name of Holistically Sound Products. Even Alyson used some of their products, not that I would ever tell her. She'd probably stop buying them if she knew.

I really hoped Alyson didn't realize where we were. Not that the witches needed her business, they were doing quite well, but I'd already bought her a gift basket for Christmas and I didn't relish the idea of getting her a new gift. Besides, I enjoyed the smell of coconut plumeria.

"Alyson, please be polite. This is important. They might have the information we are looking for." I begged with my eyes for her to go along with me on this. "You do want to solve this, right?"

"Or, they could be our murderers. Magic was used at those sites. Granted, it was dark magic but any of these witches could have gone over to the dark side." Alyson retorted.

"It wasn't the work of an organized coven. None of them would use dark magic. They haven't even attempted it in over a century so please don't accuse them of this. Let me take point while you just sit back and listen for a change. Please?" I took her hands in mine and pleaded with my eyes for her to follow my lead. "Otherwise, you may as well wait in the car."

"Fine. I'll play nice." She rolled her eyes and followed behind me to the front door.

I knocked and waited for someone to answer. Normally, I would call first but with all the phones still down, well, I just hoped they were home.

The front door creaked open. If this were a horror movie, we would be in trouble right about now. The light above the entry was flickering and all the windows were boarded up. This abandoned warehouse park had seen better days, at least according to the glamour.

Fortunately, we weren't in that kind of movie and behind the opening door was Stella, one of Mara Zoltar's daughters. "Vlad. Good of you to drop by. The great witch was hoping you would. She tried to call but, well, you know the issue with the phones. Please come in."

"Stella, good to see you too. This is my partner, Alyson Andrews." I motioned to my stony-faced partner who couldn't even muster up a polite smile before nodding to Stella. "Alyson, this is Stella, the daughter of the great witch, Mara. She's one of those who have been quite helpful in the past."

I really hoped Alyson could hold in her prejudice for just one conversation, a hope that seemed to bear fruit as she seemed to rally, giving Stella a small smile. "Nice to meet you." At least she didn't shift to her dragon form and blow fire on the poor witch.

"I should warn you, Mother is not having a good day. I actually haven't seen her this bad before. The council is talking about retiring her soon." Stella's eyes shone with unspent tears.

"I'm sorry, Stella. You mother has had a rough life. Maybe it's time she stepped down voluntarily and enjoyed life and her grandkids." I hated to hear this about my old friend. She meant a lot to me.

"Come on, maybe seeing you will help her rally."

Stella led us further into the labyrinth that was the witch's den, before we came to an old oak door that did not fit with the rest of the business decor. Someone must have changed out this door at some point. There were carvings of a forest and the moon etched into the oak. A few large stags were also carved into the scene.

Stella opened the door and bid us entry. "Mother, guess who's come to visit?"

Mara was naked and painting an ocean scene of a lone woman looking out to the sunset. The painting was actually quite good. I never knew she was an artist. To think, after all the years I had known her, I didn't know this about her.

The elderly witch turned around and I did my best to avert my eyes. Alyson stifled a groan behind me and I could see she was taking in the rest of the room instead of Mara's body.

"Mara, it's good to see you again," I said. "Would you like to get dressed and meet my partner?" If she was having an elderly moment, when she came back around it would most likely embarrass her to know we saw her like this.

"You've seen my body so many times, Vlad darling. Why should I cover up? Why, just last week we made love on the ocean. See?" She gestured grandly to the canvas. "My painting. It's of our last encounter, when you said you had to leave me."

I had not planned on letting Alyson know this part of my past, so hoping that it might snap Mara out of the moment, I said, "Mara, that was fifty-five years ago."

Stella walked up to her mother and put a black robe on the old woman's shoulders. Once the robe was secured Mara's eyes seemed to clear up. "Oh!

Vlad, you came. So good of you to come. What do you think of this business with the eco-terrorists?"

"Mara, I would like to introduce you to my partner. You remember me telling you about her, right? Alyson."

I turned around and waved Alyson over. I could tell she was extremely uncomfortable. She wouldn't look at any of us. Her eyes were focused on the painting.

"Nice to meet you, Mara. That is a wonderful painting." Alyson pointed to the work which seemed almost completed on the easel.

"Thank you, dear, it's from a simpler time in my life. What a wonderful memory." Mara looked to me and smiled. "But you didn't come here to see an old woman's painting. What can we do for you?"

Mara gestured for us to sit on a nearby couch. On a small table in front of it, an antique tea service was ready, the pot steaming as if someone had just made a fresh pot.

I took a seat on the couch and Alyson settled next to me. "I wanted to know if you knew anything about what was going on with the paranormal murders, the ones the mortals are calling the Ripper killings. We have had eleven so far, and still are no closer to finding out what happened."

"I am sad to say we do not know what's causing this. Two of my daughters and most of my coven are out right now trying to find answers." Mara sighed and seemed to drift off to another world. Knowing her age and her mental issues, she might be.

"Have you lost anyone to these murderers?" I knew witches would never report a murder of their own. Instead, they would hunt down the perpetrator and skin them alive, literally. So, it was very possible they'd lost people as well.

Mara looked at me with clear eyes which spoke to her sanity. "Yes. Mona, one of our younger members, was found murdered just a week ago. It was a ritual killing. Can you show me another site? I might be able to help if I have more information."

"Yes, I think we can," I nodded. "Just last night we were called into a fresh scene. We believe dark magic was used. Maybe you can help us to pinpoint the spells and what they want with these creatures. All of them are paranormals. Mostly shifters. We believe they did murder a vampire but we can't be sure since all we found was ash. All of the bodies have been ripped open in some form or fashion, opened up using a knife in multiple places around the body, included the carotid artery. Draining the blood must have been a necessary part of their ritual."

"Interesting," Mara said, steepling her fingers, and as she opened her mouth to say more, something exploded outside.

8

ALYSON

I heard a loud crash outside. Vlad must have too because his head twisted toward the direction of the sound.

"Did you hear that?" Vlad asked, concern leaking into his voice as his eyes flicked to me.

"Yes, sounds like there might be an issue." I took a deep breath and got to my feet slowly in order to keep from startling anyone. If something was going on, panic was the last thing we needed. "Mara, how many witches are here right now?"

Her answer was cut off by an explosion loud enough to rattle the glass in the room. The distinct vibration of magic going off burst out from the protective wards surrounding us. It almost felt like an earthquake and as I clenched my hands into fists,

Mara's painting slid off the easel and crashed to the ground.

"We only have eight sentinels here," Stella answered, worry clouding her voice as she turned to look at me. "Everyone else is out investigating the murders." She shook her head. "Who would be dumb enough to attack a witch's home, especially the great witch's home?"

"Someone who knows you have very little protection right now. Do you have cameras? Any way to see how many attackers there are and what they're carrying?" I had been quiet the entire time until I heard the break-in. Now, I was in mission mode.

Vlad nodded his thanks to me. I wouldn't leave them alone to fend off an attack. I was a professional. It was our job to protect the supernatural community from evil, no matter what I felt about the victims personally. This old lady didn't deserve to be taken and sacrificed like the others. No one did.

Stella spoke up, "Yes, down the hall is our security room. Let's head there."

"Do you have a panic room for your mother?" Surely they had somewhere safe to send the leader of their coven in case of an attack.

"No. Most people aren't stupid enough to attack us. Even with only eight sentinels, it would take a small army to get to my mother. We have this place locked up tight with magical surprises for those who aren't invited." Stella reached under the counter and produced a fully-automatic rifle. "And for those that don't, well, we have bullets. Lots of them."

I wanted to ask her where she'd gotten the AK-47, but when Stella grabbed four KA-BAR knives and strapped them to her thighs, I decided I didn't need to know. Right now, I was just glad she seemed tough. Hell, if she wasn't a witch, I would probably like her.

"Got any more I can use?" I loved a good, serrated KA-BAR, or the KA-BAR neck knife. Perfect for close quarters combat.

"Sure, take what you need." Stella pulled a duffel bag out and set it on the counter. She unzipped it and gestured at the contents. "Take whatever you want."

I nearly gasped when I noticed a blade I had on my wish list. "Is this the new Becker "Moses" Bowie? I was planning on buying this with my next paycheck." The longer blade made it great for a knife fight, especially since half the time, bullets didn't work on paranormals. Decapitation though? That worked nearly every time.

"Sure is." She looked me over for a second and nodded. "Take it. I've got others." Stella emphasized the point by strapping a sheathed sword to her back.

"Thanks," I said as Stella grabbed a satchel full of herbs. I assumed they were pre-mixed spells to be used in defense of their leader.

"Looks like someone is making a new friend." Vlad winked at me.

"Be serious." I snapped, turning toward the door. "We don't know what's coming through that door. Focus."

"Alyson's right. Fun time is over." Stella nodded to me, one hand gripping a wickedly curved kukri that gleamed in the low light.

These witches were nothing like the ones I'd crossed paths with before. Maybe it was because of their relationship with Vlad, which was something I was going to have to ask him about after this was all over with, especially since it sounded like Mara used to be his lover at one time. Sure, it could be the crazy musings of an old lady, but I doubted it. Either way though, now wasn't the time to focus on the past.

Stella opened the door to their security room right when we heard another explosion. It was getting closer. Whoever broke in was making headway. That wasn't good. While I was itching to put my new Bowie to the test, I had no idea what we were up against, and while being a dragon shifter had its advantages, going up against a grenade launcher with a knife and a pistol wasn't exactly ideal.

As Stella settled in behind an extensive monitor set-up worthy of any modern facility, she murmured, "All right, let's see who's trying to get in here."

Stella began scrolling through various images on different screens until she found her prey. "Crap! They have gotten past the first two wards." She swallowed hard. "That means they also bested three sentinels so far. Who are these guys?"

As a dozen werewolves in their shifted form appeared on screen, I felt my heart sink. This wasn't good. Not at all.

Aside from the fact that fighting a singular werewolf was hard has hell, most werewolves stood about seven feet. There were over a dozen of these guys and to make matters worse, they looked to be over eight feet tall.

Just watching them come down the hall made the Glock in my hands feel inadequate.

"We need to hurry." I gestured to the screen. "There's no way we can take on that many wolves."

"I agree." Vlad turned to the great witch. "Mara, I have to get you out of here. Is there a back exit? Someway to leave before they reach us?"

"I'm not leaving!" she shouted with surprising strength as she shoved Vlad away. "I won't leave my coven. I will stay here and accept whatever fate may bring."

I really hoped that wasn't true. While I wasn't sure what she could do against those giants, most of me knew it wouldn't be enough. Worse, there wasn't enough space in here for me to shift.

"Mother, listen to Vlad. He knows what he's talking about. You must be saved. Maura isn't ready to take over yet. Please go with them. I'll stay here and give you as much time as I can." I wasn't sure if Stella was trying to be brave, but either way, she had to know it was a suicide mission.

I shook my head. "Stella, I don't think you should stay behind. I think a trap might be better." I pointed at the screens. "That way, when they get here, they'll trigger it and bring the whole place down on themselves." I met her eyes. "Then you can come with us." I exhaled slowly. "That way, if they get to us, there will be one more in your mother's line of defense."

"Fine," Stella growled, turning fierce eyes on her mother, and despite her bravado, I could see how scared she was. It made me wondered if I looked the same. "I'll go as long as you do too, mother."

Mara glowered at her daughter for a moment, and I wanted to shake them both. We absolutely didn't have time for this. Those werewolves were getting closer by the second.

"Very well," Mara said after so long I very nearly exploded with rage.

"Finally," I said, moving toward the far door. "Let's go before we get eaten."

"Is there anything you absolutely need to take with you?" Vlad asked, and I whirled around to glare at him. Didn't he realize we didn't have time for this?

I didn't hear Mara's response because my gaze was locked on the screens. They were standing in front of a sigil-inscribed tile, and while I wasn't sure what it did, I knew it had to be a defense of some sort. A small flicker of relief hit me. Good. That'd buy us time.

Or so I thought. Before I could even tell the others about what was happening on screen, one of the wolves moved forward and stepped right on the sigil-inscribed tile. A torrent of fire obliterated him while his friends waited for the fire to put itself out. Then they walked by his charred corpse to meet another sentinel.

"Vlad, look." I pointed to the screen, one finger shaking. "They're making it here by sacrificing their own." I swallowed. "If they keep that up, they'll be here in no time."

"Then they'd better plan on sacrificing more of them. Nancy's one of our better sentinels. She may not survive this, but she will give us more time," Mara said as an invisible shield went up between Nancy and the wolves.

"Either way, we need to—"

My words were interrupted by an explosion that rocked the room as the wolf broke the barrier with a swipe of his claws. I could see his snout pulled back, growling filling the air as he stalked toward Nancy. She threw her hand toward him and the wolf caught on fire.

"He should not have been able to bring the shield down so fast." Mara narrowed her eyes and shook her head as she peered at the screen like she was trying to figure out what was going on instead of fleeing. "Someone or something has to be helping him."

"Vlad! We need to go," I snapped, tightening my grip on my Glock. "Come on."

"Mara, we don't have much time. They will be here soon." Vlad pulled Mara with him and I followed. Stella stayed behind only long enough to set the last spell before hurrying after us.

Before she caught up to us, I heard another explosion rock the place. This one was stronger than all of the rest, strong enough that it brought the false ceiling above down on us.

Vlad used his quick reflexes to protect Mara from the debris. As for me, I was pretty tough. I just put my arms above my head out of instinct more than anything. Still, as debris tumbled all around me, I was glad nothing big fell on me because even though I was a dragon shifter and had stronger skin even in my human form, a giant block would still knock me out.

As we pushed away the debris, Stella caught up to us.

I glanced at her. "Nancy?"

Stella shook her head and her eyes bored into the ceiling as she clenched her fists and took several calming breaths. "At least she took out two more wolves. Eight wolves left."

Those weren't good odds. It made me want to escape even more. Sure, witches protected their own, and if the leader of this coven, who also happened to rule the witch's council, was murdered, our city would burn as every coven in North America sought vengeance against whoever dared to attack their leader. Unfortunately, that wouldn't keep us from already being dead.

Still, as I had the thought, another popped into my brain.

"Stella, could it be another coven trying to take over?" I gestured back down the tunnel. "You saw how quickly they tore through Nancy's shield. That had to be with magic."

"No way," she answered as we pushed on. "No coven would act like this. We may not always get along, but we don't kill our own. A convicted Witch Killer is tortured until the victim begs for a death that won't easily come."

"Are you sure?" I asked. If these werewolves had magic, I wanted to be ready for it. "What about rogues? How do you explain those wolves? Think about it, Stella. They shouldn't have been able to make it through your wards or best your sentinels so easily. They have to have been amped up on magic." I wanted to say black magic, but I wanted her to say it first. If I did, she might just clam up, and that wasn't what I needed right now. I needed her to give me an edge in case those wolves got to us before we escaped.

"There is no way any witches would have helped shifters, especially to attack other witches. I'm sure you know we don't play well with others." Stella was stating it mildly.

Shifters and witches were always at each other's throats, which was one reason why I'd thought witches were involved in this case somehow. Not this coven, per se, but there has to be at least a high witch somewhere involved if black magic was involved. That combined with the level of magic being used to defeat the wards so quickly, meant there had to be someone powerful backing these wolves.

"Stella—"

"Let's just get out of here first, then we can talk about the possibility." Without another word, Stella ran ahead to help her mom, leaving me to guard the rear which was fine by me. If the wolves came at us, I wanted a chance to take them on while the others fled. Then, if they got far enough, maybe I could shift and stop them. I might not be able to go full dragon down here, but maybe I wouldn't have to. A few well-placed fireballs and some scales for armor might be enough.

"You aren't afraid of tight spaces, are you?" The wicked gleam in Mara's eyes as I turned toward her set me on edge.

"No, why?" I asked, glancing at the door set in the wall just ahead.

"We have to go through an exit tunnel which will take us to our emergency vehicles." Mara frowned. "Sorry, but you've probably lost that pretty SUV of yours."

"No worries, it wasn't ours." I shook my head.

"Good to know." Stella smirked as she opened the door, revealing what looked like a mine shaft. Without another word, she stepped through, leaving me to follow behind.

I had to bend my head to fit, and as we moved forward, the tunnel continued to shrink as we moved, walls and ceiling pressing down on us from every angle. Worse, the further we went, the more we had to hunch over to keep from hitting our heads.

Packed dirt surrounded us all the way around. Two by fours supported the walls and ceiling every few feet. It was sturdy enough to get through as long as we didn't have to turn around and fight.

"The wolves will have a problem getting through here quickly, but they will still come," I called ahead from my position in the rear. "Can we hurry it up?" I didn't want to be stuck in these tunnels fighting wolves. At this point, the height was still close to five feet. The wolves may not be able to stand erect, but they'd still be better off fighting against someone like me, given they could do it on four legs.

"I locked the door behind us with a magical spell and also put a thick, metal bar over it. If they get to the door, it will take them a while to get through. We should already be gone by the time they do."

Stella's magic had to be pretty strong if she thought her shield would hold them back for long. Either that or she was extremely confident of her abilities. While I could get behind that kind of confidence, I just hoped it wasn't misplaced, especially since I'd seen them take down the sentinel's shield in moments. Then again, Stella had seen that too.

Before we made it out, an explosion bigger than any of the others rocked the tunnel. Dirt began to fall from the ceiling and walls all around us, and as the two-by fours fought to hold the tunnel together, I wondered if I was about to be buried alive.

"Was that your trap?" I asked Stella as soon as things settled.

"Unfortunately." She took a deep breath. "I hadn't expected them to already be at the door. Still, it was a good one. While it might not have killed them all, it had to have taken care of most of them." Stella pushed forward and I followed her. "Now we just have to get out of here."

"What exactly was the trap?" I wondered aloud.

"I set magical charges all around the last room in the warehouse. Anyone without our coven's magic would automatically set it off as soon as they stepped inside the room. Those destruction spells should have brought down the entire warehouse and some of the surrounding buildings down on their heads." Stella had some serious juice if she managed that without dropping unconscious from the effort.

Just as I was thinking we were going to get out alive, another explosion rocked the tunnel, causing the section behind us to collapse.

Dirt began to rain down around us as the two by fours collapsed, and as I threw my arms up in a pointless effort to shield myself, Stella put her hands up and began chanting in Latin. Magic flowed out from her hands in a translucent green fog, causing the tunnel above us and in front of us to stay intact, at least until we moved forward. As we walked forward, the dirt behind us fell down and blocked our rear path.

That might have been a Godsend. There was no way any surviving wolves would be able to catch up to us. They would have to go around and find out where this tunnel exited. By then, we would be gone.

9

ALYSON

The tunnel led out through a small hatch into a surprisingly-well stocked garage. It was a self-contained building, maybe an old storage building. My eyes were immediately drawn to one vehicle in particular.

"Please tell me that's what we're taking." I pointed to a shiny, black Hummer. It looked like it was a second gen model, not the smaller H3.

Stella raised her brows and smiled before jumping into the driver's seat. "Well, get in. Vlad, can you get my mother situated in the backseat and sit with her? Alyson, I'll need you up front in case we come across anything you need to shoot." Stella handed me the AK-47 along with three Glocks as I slid into the seat. "In the center console should be more ammo for both."

Wow, Stella was prepared for an invasion. Just great, I actually liked this chick. Mentally, I threw my hands in the air and began to give up my hatred toward her. Little by little, she seemed to make it impossible to *not* be friends.

"We should head to the latest crime scene assuming we aren't followed. I want your mom to see if she can recognize any scent or witch signatures." I checked the ammo on all of the weapons and made sure the safeties were still on for the guns Stella handed me as well as my own.

The last thing we needed was a loaded weapon going off when we crested a hill. I was sure we would be doing some serious off-roading before we made it to the last crime scene in Palmdale.

We peeled out of the garage and into the dead of night in the high desert. Though we weren't out in the greater LA basin yet, we were about half-way down the Angeles National Forest. If we could get to Santa Clarita, we could probably lose anyone who's following us, if any of them survived the final explosion of the witch's lair.

I kept an eye out for any headlights in the rear-view mirror. It could signal we were being followed. This wasn't exactly an area known for tourists, so anyone here would most likely be after us. After we went for a few miles with no one in sight, I started to relax. We were going to get to the city.

"Do you have a safe house the rest of your coven knows about?" I knew Stella had a destination in mind, I just didn't know what it was.

Stella had slowed up on the gas over the past few miles. She must have felt like I did, we were out of danger. For the moment. "Yes. It's in the city. Any of us who survived the attack will go there, as will the rest of our family when they come back and see what happened. It's the only place in the area we have now. Thankfully, no one outside of the coven knows about it."

"Umph." I must have banged my rump at least a dozen times already on this trek. I was in pretty good shape, but riding through the desert at over forty miles an hour just wasn't good for the body, even in a Hummer.

We finally pulled out of the desert and were heading down highway 14 toward Santa Clarita. Too bad we weren't going for the roller coasters the town was so well known for. Although, this ride was like a roller coaster, just not as fun. I didn't know how Mara was handling the jerking motions of riding off-road through the desert.

"They're heeeeerrre," Mara said in a sing-song

voice which reminded me of the *Poltergeist*. Even the hairs on the back of my neck stood on end, just like when I watched the movie.

Before anyone had a chance to question the old bat, lights showed up in the rear view mirror. I should have known it was too easy to get away.

"Get ready to start shooting. We aren't far from the 5 freeway. This is going to get hairy." Stella's knuckles turned white as she tightened her grip on the steering wheel.

I wasn't going to complain about getting to kill some werewolves. These guys were definitely going to get what they deserved and more. Still, I wondered why they were after the great witch. Was it because they were connected to the other murders or for another reason entirely? I wasn't sure, but either way, they were going down.

When the car got closer, Vlad rolled down his window and hung out from behind Stella, holding his service pistol. With his side covered, I rolled my window down and hung out with the AK-47 at the ready. Between the both of us we would have no problem hitting the oncoming car and anyone inside. I only hoped I could stop them before we entered the freeway. Right now, we were traveling down a small highway which wasn't known for late night traffic. Most of the traffic on this road happened during commuter's hours so it was the best place to have a running gun battle.

"Hold on, let them get a little closer." Vlad must have wanted to get the driver before they realized what we had.

"Uh, I think you need to take that guy out now. There's someone hanging out a window on my side with a semi-automatic. Mara, lean forward and stay out of the path of stray bullets." I pulled the trigger before they were close enough.

Bullets slammed into the Dodge Charger chasing us, tearing some pretty large holes in the front fender and the windshield.

"Flames and cauldrons," I cursed. I was definitely going to have to speak to the boss about getting an AK-47 for field use.

My next burst hit the guy in the front passenger seat, spraying blood across the back of his seat as he slumped against his seatbelt. A quick glance at Vlad let me know he had emptied his weapon because he was shoving a new magazine into place. It made sense. After all, his Glock only held ten rounds while my AK-47 held thirty.

I glanced down to see Mara was still sitting upright in her seat, and saw the witch hadn't ducked down at all. Instead, she stared wide-eyed out the back window.

"Mara, please duck down so no stray bullets can get you. All of this will be for nothing if you get killed en route," I called.

"Don't worry, dear. I have my shield up. No bullets will get through." The old lady sat there like nothing was wrong. She didn't look frightened or worried. Her face was calm and she even had a small smile going. Crazy coot.

Still, that made me a bit relieved. After all Vlad and I could both take a few as long as they didn't get any important organs, and we both had accelerated healing powers. That just left Stella, but something told me she probably had a shield too.

Still, getting shot wasn't exactly fun, especially when compared to shooting the bad guys.

I leaned outside the window and took aim, while trying to dodge bullets coming from the Charger. This time, my burst only succeeded in perforating the car, but it did cause the guy who had my matching AK-47 to tuck back inside his car to save his skin.

Stella swerved back and forth, trying to give both Vlad and I good shots while keeping the enemy from hitting us too hard, but even still, as my next burst tore the fender off their car, the back window of our Hummer shattered as at least a dozen bullets came careening right for Mara.

A blue glow surrounded her, and I heard a popping sound like popcorn. Her shield protected her, sending the bullets ricocheting back out the window. Crazily, they seemed to fly back in the exact same trajectory they came flying in on.

Man, I needed to get one of those. Talk about return to sender.

"Hold on!" Stella screamed as she took the 5 freeway entrance way too fast for any car, let alone a SUV. Granted, the Hummer was weighted to be able take a good turn but even still it came up on two tires, and for a moment, I worried we were going to tip over. Only, just as we were about to tip over, white light enveloped the car, pushing it back on its wheels in a shriek of steel. As I glanced at Mara in time to see the glow fading from her hand, the tires caught with a squeal of burning rubber and we were off again.

As we careened around the corner, stray bullets took out the rear side window on my side of the Hummer. They were getting too close to hitting me. While I could heal from a bullet or two, it'd still hurt like a son of a gun. Worse, I had to stay out here if I had any hope of stopping them before they turned us into swiss cheese.

"Hang on!" Stella cried right before the Hummer lurched sideways, careening across the street.

I almost dropped the gun as I grabbed the side and held on for dear life. The second we started to straighten out, I aimed at the Dodge again. This time I hit someone leaning out to fire at us. The rounds tore into his chest, ripping him from the car and sending his bullet-riddled corpse skidding across the asphalt.

As my AK-47 went empty, another one of their guys returned fire. Before I could duck back inside, a bullet smashed into my left bicep. Agony shot through me as the AK-47 in my hands slipped from my grasp to dangle by the strap.

Ignoring it, I threw myself back into my seat and gritted my teeth as red began to soak through my sleeve. Even still, I could feel it starting to heal already, and a quick look told me why. It was a through and through. Still, I'd need to wrap my arm to keep the blood flow to a minimum.

Bullets tore through the metal frame of our vehicle as the enemy unloaded on us. The pounding noise was so loud, it reminded me of a time when hail the size of baseballs rained down on my truck while I was in Texas on an assignment.

With my excellent hearing, I would have a headache when this was all over with. The only thing keeping it at bay was the adrenaline coursing through my system.

I tore off the bottom of my shirt and wrapped the material around the hole in my arm. It wasn't pretty, but it would do. Thankfully, the pain was minimal. As long as I could keep the blood from flowing, I would heal quickly.

Another volley of bullets hit our rear quarter panel, sending it spinning off into the night. Too bad it didn't fly back and crash into the Dodge chasing us.

"Some help here would be nice," I called over to Stella. "I heard we had two of the strongest witches on the continent in the vehicle. Is there something you can do?"

I understood Stella was driving, but her mom just sat there in her magical bubble not doing anything to help. There had to be something she could do. A nice fireball would have been awesome, or maybe some form of levitation could be used to destroy the car chasing us.

Mara gave me a pointed look. "I have already

shielded the tires. Even if they aim at our wheels, they won't penetrate. There are too many people around to witness anything else I might do to help. If I broke the paranormal rules, the FBI might send someone to arrest me."

Vlad caught my eye and smirked. He wasn't going to let me live this down. I had actually asked for magical help after I told him how much I hated witches.

Taking a deep breath and forcing down the pain, I reloaded my AK-47 and waited until I could clench my hand around it once more. Satisfied, I readied myself. As soon as the bullets stopped flying, I put my upper body out the window and began shooting.

Stella weaved in and out of traffic. Thankfully, it was rather light. Between the late-night hour and the eco-terrorist attacks, most people were staying indoors tonight.

"Veer to the left so I can get a good angle on these guys," I ordered Stella.

"As soon as a pocket opens up, I will." Stella stayed in her lane for a few more seconds, slowing down before shouting, "Now!" She swerved to the fast lane, giving me an opening.

Trusting in my precise reflexes, training, and

excellent vision, I squeezed the trigger. My first round blew their windshield into a spiraling web of cracks moments before it slammed into his neck in a spray of red. The next round hit his head, blowing the rest of what remained of his life out across the seat.

The driver swerved over to the other side. The only guy left alive I could see was the driver.

"Vlad, did you take out any of them? I got two." I figured since the men were so large, they could only fit four shifters into the Charger.

"I stopped the shooter on my side. If there is a fifth in there, I can't see him. Can you?" Vlad shimmied back inside and pulled out the magazine from his gun.

"Looks like it's just their driver, now." I looked back through our broken rear window and scanned the car to see if anyone else was moving.

Other cars were trying to get out of our way. Some veered over to the slow lane and onto the side of the freeway, others just slowed down so they were behind us while a few sped up. Probably thought they could outrun us and our guns. Stupid. They should have pulled over to the side or gotten off at the next exit.

"I'm out. Hand me one of the Glocks and some

spare ammo." Vlad called out to no one in particular. "Those magazines don't match mine."

I wasn't sure if he thought Mara would give it to him or if he expected me to stop what I was doing and get him armed again. When no one moved to do as he said, he leaned back inside and picked up a loaded Glock from the front center console.

"Thanks," he grumbled.

I was almost out of ammo anyway and would have had to come back inside to reload in a few seconds. Hopefully, when I hung out the window again I could cause enough damage to force our pursuer to lose speed. Or crash. I would have preferred a crash, as long as the civilians weren't in the way.

My target would have to be their tires. From our angle, it would be tough to hit them though.

"Hit their engine, try to kill it," I yelled back to Vlad before I threw two more loaded magazines on his seat.

"I'm trying, but you're the one with the AK-47," he yelled back.

"Fair enough, I'm going to try and crash them." I leaned back out with my new magazine, the last one for the AK-47, and began firing at its engine.

The barrage of bullets blew the hood off, sending it right over the top of the Dodge. Smoke billowed out of the engine as it wheezed and coughed.

"Punch it! I think their engine's gonna blow." The smoke coming out of the front told me something was either very wrong or very right, depending on what a person wanted from this situation.

As we pulled further away from them, I shot into the engine again, unloading the rest of the clip.

It happened so fast, like something straight out of the movies. The engine blew and the driver lost control. Smoke poured out of the front of the vehicle even thicker than just a few seconds before.

The car veered toward the center divider which was a concrete barrier. The tires screeched up the concrete and more smoke covered the wheels. It looked as though the brakes didn't work or Vlad had killed the driver so his foot was still on the gas.

With no braking to stop it, the car kept going up the concrete barrier and eventually gravity took over, flipping it on its top. The metal grating on the blacktop of the freeway actually hurt my ears. Most humans wouldn't be as bothered by the sound since they did not pick up on all sound frequencies at the level shifters did. It was like someone scratching their fingernails along a chalkboard, but times one hundred.

If the driver was still alive, he had to be hurting. I hoped none of them survived this. I doubted they were the last of their rebel group but as long as no one knew what we were driving and where we were heading, we were safe.

"Did you kill them all?" Stella asked.

I turned back in my seat, facing forward as she raced down the freeway, thankful we were in a Hummer instead of my old sedan. There was no way we would have survived the firefight in an Oldsmobile. Even though the H2 was a civilian vehicle, it was built on the bones of a military SUV. It was too bad they didn't make these anymore.

"Certainly hope so," I said. "We should be safe to head to your secret house but first, I think we should make our way back to Palmdale and check out the last crime scene. Nobody would expect us to go there now. It's probably the safest time to do it." If the witches could identify the magic used, we just might be able to find the sickos responsible for these ritualistic murders.

The past twenty-four hours had been seriously intense, and normally I'd call it in, but with the phones down, I didn't want to waste the time going in. Besides, that'd probably just leave us with mounds of paperwork.

Between the latest murder scene, the biker gang, the witches, and now a freeway chase and firefight, I honestly didn't know how I was going to get through the next day if things didn't slow down.

Without the phones working, I doubted local cops would be receiving a call anytime soon about this freeway chase. As a federal agent, it was my duty to call local dispatch and let them know what just happened but without phone service, I couldn't. If I had my car still, I could have used the radio and called it in.

I couldn't control the situation, I could only hope and pray everyone got out of our way and no stray bullets hit anyone.

10

ALYSON

S tella slowed down and headed toward the freeway exit. "Where is the latest crime scene?"

"Turn around and head back up to Palmdale, exit at West Palmdale Boulevard, and I'll direct you from there," I explained. "Also, take a side road instead of getting back on the 5, at least until we pass the accident location. I don't want any possible survivors to see us heading back the way we came." I doubted there were any survivors but shifters were tough, one just never knew.

Black Hummers were very common in Los Angeles, but a black Hummer with bullet holes, busted windows, and a missing rear quarter panel would make us stand out like a sore thumb.

By the time we made it back to the crime scene, it was already after midnight. We would have to hurry up if we wanted to get Vlad indoors safely before the sun rose.

"Mara, how are you feeling? Did the jostling or the bullets hurt you?" Vlad asked as he helped the old lady down from the car.

"Don't worry about me. I'm fine. I already told you I had my shield up. It saved me the pain from the off-roading as well. Let's get this done. I'm tired. Most of us old ladies go to bed by nine." Mara giggled as she walked up to the door and waited for us.

I shook my head, looking to Stella. "Your mom is kinda crazy. You do know this, right?"

Stella suppressed a laugh. "Yup, and I wouldn't have her any other way. I just hope I'm half as spry when I'm her age."

"Preach it." It would be good for anyone to have as much energy as Mara when they were in their seventies. For me, seventy would still be young so I better still have a ton of energy. Dragons were supposed to live for several hundred years, if they weren't hunted down and murdered.

Vlad pulled the police tape aside and opened the door. "Mara, please try not to disturb anything in the house, if you can help it. Even though photos have been taken and evidence collected, you never know when the techs need to come back for something new."

"It's not my first crime scene. I've been called in to assist with too many murders to count. Stand back and let me work." A purple glow emanated around Mara's body and she closed her eyes.

Mara's lips were moving, but I couldn't hear any words. She seemed to be chanting something. Since it wasn't audible, I wondered if she was just meditating to get in the mood, considering most witches needed to say their incantations aloud in order for them to work. Only a handful could silently speak the words to make a spell work.

Was Mara one of those?

If so, she was a very powerful witch. It could be why the werewolves showed up at the witch's lair. Now that I thought about it, they couldn't have known we were there. It may have been fate that brought us to her lair. I doubt they would have gotten away if Vlad and I hadn't been there to help.

The glow around Mara changed to red and her hands moved in a circle in front of her. She picked something out of her satchel and threw it into the ritual room.

"Flames and Cauldrons. I hope she didn't just contaminate the crime scene with some herbs." I shook my head and prayed whatever she was doing wouldn't leave any evidence or trace of her presence.

"Don't worry," Stella murmured, all her attention on her mom. "She's performing a spell to uncloak any incantations which were performed here. Once she's all done, the ingredients she just used will disappear. The goddess will take them as an offering to her realm."

I looked to Vlad and raised my eyebrows and mouthed, "Goddess?"

Vlad put a finger up to his lips and mouthed, "Shh."

These people and their crazy beliefs. I knew witches worshipped something other than God, but to hear them talking about it was just freaky.

All at once, the entire house lit up with a white light so bright, I could hardly see. As it dissipated, I could see characters in the air hovering over the spot where the dead body was discovered. After a moment, those characters resolved into words, mostly in Latin or at least I thought it was Latin. I didn't speak anything other than English and a few phrases in conversational Russian thanks to Vlad's lessons.

I wanted badly to ask questions. Something inside told me to keep quiet and wait. My time to ask questions couldn't be too far off.

Another pop sounded, almost like a gunshot, and I looked around before realizing the aura surrounding Mara had disappeared. She slouched onto the ground, and both Vlad and Stella ran for her.

"Mother, are you all right?" Stella held her mother's head in her lap while Vlad checked her pulse.

"Yes, dear. I'm fine. Just tired. I did tell you it was way past my bedtime, didn't I?" Mara must have been feeling decent to be cracking jokes.

Stella and Vlad helped her up.

"So, what does this all mean? I saw the Latin scrolling through the air over the crime scene." I bit my lip in anticipation of some answers.

"It means you were right. It's black magic. I know this spell. Let's leave and I'll tell you all about it." Mara stepped out of Stella's arms and made for the front door.

"Wait, let me go first, just to be safe." I went outside and scanned the area to ensure it was safe.

"Come on, let's get out of here." Vlad took Mara by the arm and led her to the Hummer.

Stella had cast a protective spell on the vehicle to ensure no one messed with it while we were inside. "It's clear. No one touched it."

As soon as we were back on the 14 freeway, I turned around and looked at Mara. "Well?"

Mara narrowed her eyes and looked out the front window. "I didn't realize anyone even knew this spell. It should have died when I was just a girl. The council of that time outlawed it and made it a worldwide law. Anyone caught even looking into this spell would receive instant death. There are no second chances for disobeying this law."

"Is there any sort of spell book that would still have it listed?" I wasn't up on all of the witch's lore or laws, or even what they did, but how could a spell be lost if it was known only sixty years ago? Someone, somewhere would still have it listed, possibly in an old book or inside a safe.

"The council ordered every witch to destroy any evidence of this spell, and then they had each coven leader question their members about it. All covens swore an oath stating everyone who had any knowledge had destroyed it. Either someone went rogue, which is almost unheard of, or a book which had been long forgotten was recently unearthed with the spell." Since Mara was the leader of her coven as well as the North American council, she would most likely be honor-bound to find the individual who cast it.

"What does the spell do?" Vlad asked what was on my mind.

"It destroys the world."

Vlad looked at me with wide, redeyes. He was always the calm, collected one, but now, he looked like he was about to shift into his vampiric form. I didn't mind his red eyes and fangs, but I knew he hated for others to see him lose it.

He looked out his side window and sat silently.

"Are you saying someone actually created a spell to end the world? How is that possible?" My headache was coming on. Forget the adrenaline rush from earlier, the dread of what's actually happening was going to kill me.

"I am sworn to secrecy. However, you should know what the outcome would be should they complete the spell." Mara looked down at her trembling hands. I hadn't seen this woman so much as sweat since I met her. Bullets were ricocheting off her and she smiled. Her obvious fear was working to put me into a panic attack.

"What? Do they summon an asteroid or something? A planet-killer?" It had happened before. The dinosaurs are extinct from what was assumed to be an asteroid. It could happen again.

"No. The spell opens the veil between our world and Hell. All of the demons waiting for the dead will be unleashed here on Earth. No one would survive for long."

I did not expect that one.

"So, Hell is real? We're looking at a Biblical end-of-the-world scenario and all that kind of stuff? Plagues and horsemen of the apocalypse type of days, is that what we have to look forward to?" I've read the Bible, I know what it says. I just didn't think it was real. Still don't if I'm honest with myself.

There had to be another possibility, like an alternate dimension. I have met a few very intelligent humans who believe demons are just paranormal creatures from another reality.

The FBI even has a team of scientists who were studying the Multiverse Theory. While I wasn't a scientist, one of my previous partners was. He explained this possibility to me and it actually made sense. We just couldn't prove it yet. If demons made it here via this magical spell, it just might be what we needed to prove it, which sounded like the only silver lining to the whole thing.

"Those who survive the plagues would wish for death during the initial onslaught." Mara was all doom and gloom, just what we needed.

"What about magic? Could your kind help keep it at bay?" Mara was the strongest witch I had ever heard of, surely she could do something.

"No. Even if there were hundreds of me here on Earth, we couldn't stop it once it starts. Our best bet is to stop the ritual before they finish it. The blood of one hundred paranormal creatures are needed for it. Based on what you told me and those I have lost, they must have at least twenty-five rituals completed by now." It was a good thing Mara was on our side or else we would still be grasping in the dark for clues when the apocalypse happened.

"Mother, I think it's time," Stella said cryptically. "I know you don't like them, but we need their help."

"Who's help?" Vlad asked.

"Without a phone, we can't reach out to the other covens of the world very easily. With enough witches, we could reach one or two covens telepathically and let them know what's going on. In order to have enough strength, I need another coven leader." Mara glared at Vlad with cold, hard, meaningful eyes.

"You don't mean those nutcases in Venice? Surely, you could do this without them, right?" Vlad let out a deep breath and put his head in his hands.

"Hello! New to the group here. Who's in Venice?" I wasn't following what they were talking about. Some nutcase in Venice? Didn't we already have a nutcase in the Hummer?

Mara turned her gaze towards me. "There is a second coven in Southern California. Normally, witches don't live very close to each other, but this is an unusual case. About a hundred years ago, my coven split into two factions. One wanted to live more in harmony with the Earth and the other wanted more power."

She sighed softly. "The group who wanted more power moved to the beach and kept to themselves. They limited their coven size so they wouldn't stand out or have to share power with too many others. Ironically, in doing so, they ended up losing power. You see, in order to increase the magical power inherited between generations, a coven needs new blood. The Venice coven weakened their bloodlines by inter-marrying too much."

The old lady's eyes shimmered with unshed tears. "Stella, go ahead and take us to Eliza. Either way, they need to know what's going on. Their entire coven is in danger."

"I'm going to try calling base, again," I said as I pulled out my cellphone. "Maybe I'll get lucky this time." Unfortunately, it was the same as before, it just rang and rang. I wondered if we were ever going to be able to contact anyone.

"Anything?" Vlad inquired.

"Nope, nothing. Maybe tomorrow? Either way, we have to get you to cover soon. After we check in with Eliza, we need to find a place for Vlad to rest during the day. Can we make it back to your safe house before the sun rises?" My entire life revolved around the sunset and sunrise, so I was very attuned to the sun and moon cycles.

Stella checked her watch. "Yes, we should have time. I doubt we'll be visiting long with the Venice coven. They don't like us very much." She chuckled.

"How will they feel about a vampire and a shifter who work for the FBI coming over?" The last thing we needed was a confrontation with a psycho witch coven.

"I think you'll be more welcome than we will," Mara grunted.

"Joy. Let's get this over with." I wasn't looking forward to meeting the rest of Mara's coven, let alone one Vlad didn't even like based on his reaction to the news.

11

ALYSON

Stella pulled up to a large warehouse only a few blocks from Muscle Beach. I'd been by here before and never realized it was owned by witches. In fact, I didn't think I'd ever seen witches in Venice. If they had a coven here, I wondered why I had never sensed them.

The building was a standard, nondescript warehouse with a front store or office set-up. The walls were all concrete with a beach design imprinted on the sides, like on all the major freeways in LA. A sign out front said, "California Beach Apparel." I knew the label. I think I even had a few of their t-shirts. One of my bikinis was definitely from them, not that I had much free time to spend at the beach.

"Vlad, it might be best if you knocked on their door. A good-looking man might get them to open up. I doubt they would open it for me." Mara grimaced.

"Your wish is my command." Vlad laughed, causing Mara to narrow her eyes at him. He walked up to the door while we all stayed off to the side. When he knocked, the door creaked open slowly, as if it wasn't locked or even closed tight.

I picked up the scent of blood as Vlad shifted to his vampiric form.

"Something's wrong," he growled right before he dashed inside.

"Vlad! Get back here! It's dangerous to enter a witch's lair without permission," I called, glancing at Mara. "Is it even safe to follow him?"

"Let me check." Mara looked around and then closed her eyes for a moment. "There are no wards up, though I sense the black magic. It's all over the warehouse, like the stench of death."

"Vlad, is everything okay?" I strained my hearing to listen for any sounds, other than Vlad.

Mara shook her head and moved forward, slowly. "No, only death."

"Stella, stay with your mom. I'm going to look for Vlad. Something is off and he's my partner." I took off at a run down the dank hallway, following the sound of Vlad's growling. The walls had once been covered in cheery, floral wallpaper but now were stained and falling down in multiple places.

Sensing where Vlad was, I took the next left which emptied into a small room. There was blood and gore all over the room. I counted fifteen dead bodies, they all had been sacrificed. It was evident from the wounds on their bodies and the set-up of the room, just like the other crime scenes.

My partner was standing in the middle of a pentagram with the corpse of a young woman in his arms. The blood inside the pentagram was dry and cracked though the bodies looked like they were still somewhat fresh.

The body in his arms was still in rigor mortis, which meant they died less than two days ago. Could have been a few hours, but with the way the stench of death hung in the air. I would bet good money the bodies were starting to decay and would come out of rigor soon.

"Vlad, put her down. You're contaminating the crime scene."

I watched as Vlad looked over at me as if seeing me for the first time. Then he seemed to realize what he was doing.

"It's Sylvie," he said, taking a deep breath. "I knew her when she was a baby."

He started to say more but then just stopped and looked at the corpse in his arms. My heart ached for him, and as I tried to think of what to say, he shook his head.

I sensed movement behind me. It was Mara and Stella.

"What happened?" Stella murmured as she stayed in the doorway and eyed the room. "Does this mean witches might be exactly what we need to stop them?" I wondered glad to have something to focus on besides Vlad's pain. I wasn't sure if that made me a horrible person or not, but it sure felt like it.

"Not everyone is here." Mara walked inside the room and went to the far corner. "There were about thirty in this coven." She waved her hand through the air. "I don't sense any others though. I hope the rest are somewhere safe. Poor Eliza." Stella said, moving forward and kneeling next to another woman. "She just took over for her dead mother last year."

"This has to be stopped," Mara said, moving next to her daughter, and for a second I thought the older woman was going to comfort her daughter. Instead, she balled her hands into fists. "To think this has been happening..." she shook her head before meeting Stella's eyes. "I can't let this happen to you." With those words, Mara pulled a blood stained scarf off from around the dead woman's neck.

I rubbed my face as Mara stood and marched out of the room without a word.

"We need to call this scene in. Who knows if there are any new clues here? Damn, we've contaminated the entire scene, especially Vlad." I hoped the phones would come back on today. We needed help.

"All right, we need to leave and get somewhere safe before the sun comes up. I really don't feel like spending the day here." Vlad was actually shivering as he walked out of the room to follow Mara.

"I guess there's nothing else to do here if we can't disturb the bodies," Stella said, looking at me as she stood. When I nodded, she sighed. "It feels wrong to just leave them."

"It won't be for long," I said, wishing I believed that. With the phones down, emergency services were no doubt tied up with all sorts of things. It'd be a while before they came here, and that was assuming we could contact them anytime soon. With Vlad needing to get somewhere dark, that seemed even more unlikely.

"I hope you're right," Stella said, exiting the room.

"Me too," I mumbled, sweeping my gaze over the room before heading back to the Hummer.

Looking at the bullet-riddled vehicle, I glanced back at Mara. "Shouldn't we ditch this and grab a different vehicle? Do you think this coven has any left?" We were going to stand out badly if we kept the Hummer and it would certainly compromise their safe house.

"I doubt you will like what they have but we can see." Stella took the lead, taking us around back to what looked more like a fruit stand than a garage. It was a makeshift wooden structure that must have housed their cars.

The door was unlocked and partially open. Whoever left did so in a hurry. The first thing to catch my eye was the box of keys strewn on the ground. Most of the key chains had plastic flowers in various colors attached.

When I lifted my eyes, I groaned. The only cars left were two van conversions. One was most definitely a flower child van. It was covered in multi-colored daisies. The other looked like the Mystery Machine from *Scooby-Doo* with red, blue, and yellow blobs all over it. Painted on the side of the van facing me was, "Venice Beach Love." I don't think I wanted to know what they did with the van.

"Isn't there something better we can take? We'll stand out like a sore thumb in either of these monstrosities," I whined.

"It's either those," Stella pointed to the Sixties van conversion, "or the shot up Hummer."

"Either way, we stand out. I say let's stick with the Hummer. Even in its current shape, it will offer a lot more protection than either of these." I sighed. "Vlad's masculinity just might be called out if he was caught riding in one of those."

"I agree. Let's get moving." Stella nodded. "I'll get mom to weave a glamour over it anyway so it doesn't seem so beat up."

"You can do that?" I quirked an eyebrow at her as we made her way back.

"I can't, but mom is a master when it comes to glamour spells. She can practically hide in plain sight." She bit her lip. "This might be a bit tough for her though since we'll be moving."

I was about to say something, but before I could, she ducked into the back seat and began talking to Mara.

"Stella, you gonna keep driving?" I asked as I

approached the hummer, wondering if I should get behind the wheel.

"Yes." She poked her head out and nodded to me before moving to the front. "I know exactly where we're going. Keep an eye out in case we're spotted. Mom is gonna try with the glamour, but it will take a lot of concentration."

"Okay," I said, sliding into the passenger seat and buckling in.

It took her a couple of tries to start the engine. This beast wasn't going to last much longer.

I patted the dashboard. "Poor thing. If I could fix you, I would. Thank you for your service and protection tonight."

Stella snickered and moved us along once the engine roared to life. It never hurt to show a vehicle some love and attention.

12

VLAD

I sighed. Part of me didn't even understand why I'd dashed in there when I'd smelled the blood. After all, the women I was with didn't need protecting, but at the same time, I was just wired that way.

Still, I hadn't been prepared for what I'd seen and now every time I closed my eyes, I saw Sylvie's corpse as it lay sprawled and cut up in the house. I could still remember when I'd first met her, how vibrant and full of life she'd been. I know it sounds lame, but I had taught her to ice skate because she'd never been before. It'd seemed silly at the time, but as I thought back to the memory, her smile haunted me.

It was pathetic, and if I wanted to catch these

guys, I had to focus. Memories of the past wouldn't help me, wouldn't help Sylvie. No, only justice would help.

It was hard though. There had been so much death, and while I'd seen people die throughout the years, this case was starting to affect me more than normal.

I know that makes me sound like a heartless jerk, but it was the truth. The worst thing was, I didn't know why. Sure, I'd known Sylvie as a baby, but I'd known lots of people. No, there was something else at play here, something I didn't quite understand.

"Stella, can you hurry it up? I can feel the sun rising already, and these windows aren't going to block out the light." As I said the words, part of me was angry at myself. While I knew that I would be going up in smoke if we didn't get inside soon, I felt terrible for thinking about myself.

"Don't worry, we're only two blocks away." Stella smiled at me through the rearview mirror and turned left down a residential street.

"Your safe house is an actual house? In Compton?"

Though the streets were deserted, it was still

quite early and Compton was known for gangs and violence. I was shocked these women decided to have their "safe" house here. It was anything but. Still, even the gangs must have learned to stay away from witches.

Alyson's gaze was on the rows of houses as we passed them. "My grandma used to own a dress shop here in Compton. Back when it was a nice, little suburban town. I can't believe it was over seventy years ago that families used to safely hang out together in their front yards. Man, how things change."

I found it hard to believe this was once an idyllic little suburb. Alyson shook her head slightly as she asked the witches, "Are you sure your house here is safe from the neighborhood? Even I wouldn't dare run around here at night." She looked back at me. "Would you?"

"Blood is blood. As long as they aren't doing drugs, I'd drink anyone here who agreed." I could feel my fangs begin to elongate and my vision turn red at the thought of a woman offering up herself to please me.

What no one here knew was that I did enjoy this small town for a few years. Back in the seventies, I had a little house here. The women came and went from my pad while the men stayed away from me. I figured they knew I was different and didn't want to mess with me.

Things were different here these days. It wasn't safe for kids to play outside anymore. Too bad our suspected murderers didn't sacrifice gang members instead of paranormal creatures.

"Here we are." Stella pulled into a driveway and used her magic to open the garage door.

The garage wasn't attached to the house and it was small, really small, a wooden structure with yellow siding and white trim. It matched the house it was next to. This vehicle was going to take up the entire space.

The house had a small front enclosed porch. If I had to guess, the entire place was no larger than 1,200 square feet. It was a tiny square. The front yard had brown grass with patches of green throughout while a white picket fence which had seen better days surrounded the property.

I was sure this was a nice house when it was built but it just wasn't kept up. Neither were most houses in the neighborhood. The witches were smart. No one would come looking for a wealthy group of women in a neighborhood overrun by gangs.

That said, we would be lucky if we didn't hear gun shots later today.

Alyson was scanning the garage with wide eyes. "Why don't you let us out before you park it? I doubt we'll be able to get out once you pull in."

"Don't worry, we will have plenty of space." Mara smirked as Stella slowly inched the Hummer forward.

My stomach lurched and everything around me twisted. I felt as though I had gone down the rabbit hole. While I knew we hadn't drank any potion or eaten any cake, the garage either grew or we shrank.

"It's enchanted. The entire property is actually much larger than it looks on the outside and the wards make humans instinctively stay clear of it too. Most will even cross the street instead of walk on our side-walk." Stella could have told us that before we entered the garage. Maybe prepared us for the strange feeling.

"I understand why they stay clear now," Alyson mumbled. "This is truly a safe house. Even I don't want to be here. My head is telling me to run and my stomach is all ... hold on, I'm going to puke."

Alyson scrambled out of the Hummer and bent over like she was going to do just that. Before I could move to help her, Stella got out and rubbed Alyson's back. "Don't worry, the feeling will pass. Our wards just need to get a feel for you and realize you are welcome here. It's like a living entity. It knows who should be here and who shouldn't. It will only take another minute or so and you will be right as rain."

I walked around the Hummer and saw that there was more than enough room to park another vehicle here. "Mara, if the rest of the coven shows up with multiple vehicles, the garage will make room for it, won't it?"

"I'm impressed that you picked up on the enchantment. Yes. In fact, we can hold as many cars as we have. This garage has never turned away one of our vehicles. I have seen over fifty cars and two RV's in here before." The great witch had put one crazy spell on this place.

"How do I get from the garage to the house? I can see the orange of the sunrise already filtering between us and the house." I really hoped I wouldn't be stuck in the garage all day.

"We have an underground tunnel. Follow me."

Stella led us to the back of the garage where there was a trap door on the ground.

"I'm going through the side entrance, basements are not for me anymore. See you later today, Vlad." Mara waited for me to drop down into the tunnel before I heard her open the door.

The tunnel wasn't dank, although it was dark.

"Light." Stella cast a spell and the lamps along the walls lit up, chasing the shadows away.

The path was compact dirt below us. I could smell more dirt behind the wood covered walls. Above us, more wood covered the earth. I wondered if they dug this themselves or if it was another spell.

"Tonight, when I get up I want to see about contacting base again. We might have to just head over there if we can't reach them soon." Alyson seemed worried we couldn't reach anyone. The blasted eco-terrorists had some really bad timing with their attack on the telephone infrastructure.

"We probably should take a trip there soon," I agreed. "Stella, do you have a TV here? I want to get some news before I head off to sleep. The local early morning news shows usually have the best coverage." On a normal day, I would watch the *Wake Up California* show before I went to bed.

We all went inside the house which, like the garage, was much larger than it appeared from the outside. They had decorated it with pale yellows and blues giving the place a cozy feel.

If I didn't need the news so badly, I would have crashed on the couch as soon as I sat down. To say I was exhausted was an understatement.

Thankfully, the news was already on when we entered the room. Mara sat on the edge of a recliner with her eyes glued to the TV. "So, what's going on?" I asked.

Mara glanced at me before going right back to the news. "It looks like the eco-terrorists have targeted businesses owned by witches and other paranormal creatures."

The reporter was going over the various businesses which had been burned down overnight. "With the telephones out of service, our news is traveling to us the old-fashioned way, by Pony Express." The newscaster laughed at his own lame joke.

His fellow newscaster, a lady named Jessica, rolled her eyes as she picked up with her part of the news. "We can't say for certain that this is the complete list but as far as we can tell, fifty local businesses with ties to The Sampson Corporation and

Moonlight Incorporated have all been destroyed. The eco-terrorist group responsible for the attack on our telecommunications system has claimed responsibility for these attacks as well."

She seemed to be reading now, paraphrasing some written statement. "Their leader stated in his manifesto the CEO's of both corporations are guilty of polluting our environment with their manufacturing practices as well as with their corporate greed."

Her colleague arched an eyebrow. "I thought both companies were certified green? They worked very hard to do as little damage to our environment as possible. Could it be they lied to us, Jessica?"

"Donny, I don't think so. I wouldn't be surprised if these terrorists made up these accusations in order to justify what they are doing. It's probably a group of disgruntled former employees." Jessica narrowed her eyes and looked into the camera. "Stay tuned for more information after your local weather report."

"Wonderful." Alyson plopped on the couch next to me and heaved a heavy sigh. "It sounds like all of our problems are tied together."

I nodded in agreement. "I knew the timing of these terrorist attacks was suspicious. So, the terrorist group is run by the werewolves or are they being manipulated by them? Both of those companies are controlled by paranormals. Isn't Sampson run by bear shifters?"

"Yep and witches run Moonlight Incorporated. This was one very well planned attack. Whoever is behind this is both extremely smart and powerful, otherwise they wouldn't have been able to take down our wards and sentinels so quickly, even if they were willing to sacrifice themselves. I've never met a werewolf smart enough to come up with a plan like this, let alone execute it so flawlessly." Alyson was right, it had to be someone using the wolves.

"I agree, wolves just aren't capable of this. Whoever is behind this has magical abilities and knowledge of a ritual thought to have been destroyed over fifty years ago. Wolves don't have that kind of magical knowledge," Stella added.

"There must be a group of witches who have gone rogue. No one else could do this, could they?" Alyson asked.

Alyson had thought it was witches from early on but the pentagram was a dead giveaway. Why would witches repeatedly leave such an obvious clue?

Mara sat back in her chair, rubbing her temples as she added herself to our discussion. "No, I think there is something else we haven't considered yet. Witches would not do this, plus they are too smart to leave evidence of magic use at the crime scenes."

Mara's position and experience as the grand witch seemed to hold enough sway with Alyson for her words to actually break through her prejudice. "Okay, well, who else has magical abilities? Could a group of humans obtain magic? If they found a book of spells, would they be able to wield them?" Alyson asked.

Mara tapped her chin while looking at the TV. "I'm sorry, dear, but humans wouldn't be able to use magic unless a witch imbued them with the power. I suppose it's possible a group of halflings discovered who they were, got together, and are now getting back at the covens who created them."

"Halflings?" Alyson quirked an eyebrow questioningly. "Like in those fantasy books and movies?"

"No, a halfling is a child born to a female human who was impregnated by a male witch or mage as some like to be called," Mara explained as she slowly got to her feet. "If the mother had come from a halfling herself and she gave birth to a mage's child, it is possible they would develop power. It's very unlikely but has happened. Usually, those children are taken in by the father and his coven." As she finished her explanation, she headed to the kitchen. "Anyone want some tea?"

"Yes, please," Alyson said as she stood up to help Mara.

As Stella followed them into the kitchen, I hesitated. "Are all of the windows covered? I don't need to be hit by a stray sunbeam. It will zap what energy I have left, assuming it doesn't kill me outright."

I could withstand some sunlight as long as it was indirect, however, I would need to feed if it happened. Given what had happened earlier, something told me Alyson wouldn't be so happy to help this time.

Mara poured water into a tea pot and turned on the stove. "Yes, I closed everything in the house while you were making your way here. Don't worry, you're safe."

Relieved, I stepped into the kitchen as Alyson leaned against the counter beside Mara.

"So, it is possible we're dealing with witches, well, hybrid ones, most likely a group who were abandoned by their coven?" Alyson mused.

"Possible, but not likely," Stella mused as she

pulled a selection of tea bags down from a kitchen cabinet. "There are other species who could wield magic. Dragons for one. Fae are another possibility. Neither are very likely. The fae come from the earth and would never try to destroy it, plus demons are their natural enemies. No fae would ever want to bring demons into this world."

My eyes flicked to Alyson as I chewed on the new information. While I was certain it hadn't been her behind the murders, Stella had a point. If it wasn't witches, at least one from the main covens, and it wasn't fae or dragons, what else could it be? It stood to reason that the only thing behind it would be a Halfling, but still... how could one get powerful enough to take on the great witch's coven? That didn't add up.

"Yeah, I agree about the fae. Too much iron in the air for them to do this kind of magic anyway, and dragons are extinct," Alyson said resolutely as she wrung her hands. Her nervousness was obvious. I hoped my partner wouldn't get overly excited and blow her cover. She needed to calm herself.

"Yes, dear. I suppose they are." Mara's eyes lingered on Alyson a few seconds too long.

If anyone had the power to ascertain a shifter's other form, it would be Mara. I tried to think back to see if Alyson had given anything away. She hadn't shifted since we had joined Mara. Still, for their own sake, I really hoped Mara and Stella believed Alyson was anything other than a dragon. If they didn't, it was going to open a whole new can of worms. After all, dead men tell no tales.

Once the tea was finished, all the women fixed themselves cups. While I could drink tea if I wanted to, I just wanted to sleep.

"All right, I think it's time I went to bed. Alyson, you should get some sleep as well. It looks like we're going to have another very long night. Where is a room I can stretch out in?"

It would be better if I didn't sleep in a room with any of them. If I woke up suddenly and one of them was close, I just might steal a drink from their neck.

"You can take the back room, it's the furthest from the front of the house, in case we get an influx of witches from our coven today. Are you still scary when woken up early?" Mara had seen what happens long ago. I had never hurt her but she'd still earned more than a few accidental bite marks.

Alyson shrugged and took a sip of her tea. "Yes, he is. There should be a sign saying, 'Danger, wake upon pain of vamp feeding.'"

"I'm not that bad." I turned and went to find my room.

Later tonight we would need to see about getting some backup from command. I only hoped we could reach them via phone instead of having to drive all the way there.

13

ALYSON

"Come here, Alyson, and be a dear. I could use some help with this spell." Mara had laid the scarf belonging to the leader of the Venice coven out on the counter.

"What did you need?" I couldn't do magic, surely she knew that.

"There's a mortar and pestle in the cupboard above the microwave. Will you get it down for me?" Mara may have been old but she could have pulled this down using her magic. No, she wanted something from me. Worry flashed through me. Was she on to me? Did she know my secret?

I wasn't sure, but I kept an eye on her the best I could and reached up to pull out what she requested. "Is this what you were looking for?" I took out the mortar and pestle and laid them on the counter.

"Yes, yes. Thank you, dear." Mara patted my cheek, and I felt a strange sensation running through my body.

I took a few steps back from her as my eyes widened. What did she just do? If she tried to put a spell on me, I don't care how innocuous, she would be dead.

I narrowed my eyes at her and prepared to attack. "What did you just do?"

"Nothing much. I just needed a little bit of shifter magic for this spell. No need to worry." She waved me off like I was a little girl who had overreacted which made me even angrier.

Something about the way she said it made me think she wasn't telling me the whole truth, and while I knew she wasn't all there all the time, I was starting to think the old bat was wilier than anyone gave her credit. Worse, if she did something to expose me, I wasn't sure what I'd do. My first impulse would be to silence her and the coven, but if I did that, I wasn't even sure the FBI could save me from the retribution of the other covens, especially since I didn't technically exist.

"You should never take anything from someone

without asking," I snarled, putting my hands on my hips. "If you do it again, I don't know what I'll do, but it won't be pleasant."

"What happened?" Stella ran into the kitchen, eyes fixed on me. "I heard you raise your voice. What's going on?"

"Your crazy mother just stole some magic from me without even asking! What is wrong with you people?" I turned to leave when Stella stopped me.

"Wait. I'm so sorry. My mother knows better than to take without asking." She turned to her psycho mom. "Mother, why didn't you just ask? If you needed more power, I would have easily given it to you. We don't do this, especially to our friends."

"She doesn't need it. Look at her! She's drowning in magic and doesn't even know it. I can see it flying around her in circles, begging to be released. I did her a favor." Mara went back to making her potion, whatever it was for.

"What is your mom doing? Why is she messing with a dead person's scarf or is it part of her crazy act?" By now I wasn't so sure she was as crazy as everyone believed.

"It's a locator spell. If the person, or persons, who killed the Venice coven left any trace elements on the scarf, we can track them with the spell Mom is making. She's right though. It does take a lot of power. I am sorry she took from you in such a way. It's not our normal way, I swear." Stella seemed genuine. Her mother, on the other hand, still seemed off.

"Don't touch me again," I warned, eyes narrowed. "I'm going to find a room near Vlad to sleep. For your sake, you'd better not try anything again."

I needed to get away from these freaks. Trying to be friendly to witches was wearing me out. Just when I dropped my guard, BAM! They proved why I hated them so much.

Grumbling, I made my way toward the room they'd given me at the back of the house, but as I reached for the doorknob, something exploded. The entire house seemed to shake and as bits of plaster rained down around me, I spun on my heel ready for action. Only, no attack came, and none of the defensive wards painted along the walls flared to life. No, something else had happened.

"Did the spell go wrong?" I mumbled, and after casting a quick glance at Vlad's door to see if he'd awakened, I made my way back to the kitchen.

I walked into the kitchen and found Mara sitting on the floor beside the counter. She was covered from head to toe in viscous green goo, and her hair stood on end like that crazy scientist in *Back to the Future*.

"What happened?" I asked, torn between concern and annoyance as I made my way over to her.

"Just a bit too much power, dear. I guess I shouldn't have siphoned from you." Mara blinked her large eyes a couple times. "Your magic doesn't seem to be very compatible with mine."

As she spoke, I watched her, looking for clues that she knew my identity, but it didn't seem like she had. That left me with two options. Assume she was an uncannily good liar or that she didn't know. For the moment, option two seemed more reasonable. After all, option one led to some consequences I wanted to avoid if at all possible, especially given what seemed to be at stake with the dark magic rituals.

"Glad to see you're okay!" Stella huffed, and I turned to find her standing right behind me with her hands on her hips. "But this is exactly why we don't take magic from outside of our own coven." She sighed, shaking her head as she passed by me. "Come with me to the bathroom, and I'll clean you up."

"Guess, I'll just wait out here then," I grumbled, moving to the living room. While I'd been ready to sleep before, now I was wired, but thankfully the room had its own television. Picking up the remote, I turned it on, flipping through the channels before I settled on a mindless sitcom.

ONE MOMENT I was being massaged by a hot cabana boy on some distant shore, and the next someone was knocking on my door.

"Come in. I'm awake," I called, stretching as I glanced out the window. It was well after dark. Man, how long had I been asleep?

Vlad carefully opened the door, a steaming mug of what I hoped was coffee in his hand. "Hi. I brought you some coffee. I thought you might need it." Vlad handed me the coffee which I greedily accepted – cream and sugar, just the way I liked it.

"Thanks," I said, looking him over as he settled against the far wall. Before this case, I wasn't drawn to him, but now I was. I tried to shake it off, but yeah, jumping him looked really good right now.

"You're welcome." Vlad looked at the floor. "So, what do we do now?" He spread his hands.

"We still can't call into HQ, and we don't exactly have any leads."

"I'm not sure." I took a sip of my coffee, letting the warmth seep into me as I thought. "When people mess with things they don't understand, crazy consequences develop. There has to be a way to trace that."

"You might be right..." He stood up and walked to the door before turning to look at me.

"What's up?" I said, sitting up on the bed. Part of me was glad I'd fallen asleep in my clothes, but most of me just wanted a shower even though I knew it wasn't a good use of time now that I wasn't waiting for Vlad to wake up. I guess in retrospect, I should have ditched the sitcom and taken a shower last night. Still, I was mature enough to put the case first, even though I didn't want to.

"Nothing." He hesitated, looking like he wanted to say more.

"Nothing?" I raised an eyebrow at him. "It doesn't seem like nothing."

"Well, here's the thing..." He looked at the ceiling. "The witches came up with a plan to trap whoever is doing this."

"I thought you said we didn't have any leads?" I asked, unsure how I felt about that. On one hand, witches still rubbed me the wrong way, but on the other, well, I sort of trusted Stella and Mara. Geez, how could I even think that?

"I don't like their plan. I am hoping you'll agree." He sighed as I stood up and gulped the coffee. Even though I'd slept more than usual, I still felt drained, and this conversation wasn't helping.

"Well, with that opening, I can't wait to see what you follow with." Instead of responding, Vlad simply nodded and walked out, leaving me alone in the room.

I appreciated it, but it wasn't like I had any clothes to change into or anything, so I settled for running my hand through my hair a couple times before I left. It wasn't much, but it'd have to do.

When I entered the living room, I found Vlad chatting with Mara and Stella while ten other witches filled every other nook and cranny of the place. Vlad was right, if the plan involved this many witches, I definitely wasn't going to like it.

"Alyson! You're up! It's about time." Stella chuckled. "I wanted to go wake you but Vlad said it would be almost as bad as waking him up."

"Pfft. I'm nowhere near as bad as Vlad." I rolled my eyes. "I need more coffee before you bring me up to speed."

Some Tylenol or breakfast would have been good, too.

"There's more in the kitchen, along with eggs, bacon, and toast if you're hungry. Help yourself," Mara said, gesturing toward the kitchen.

As I entered the kitchen, Vlad walked up behind me and stood way too close for comfort, shooting tingles of lust through my veins. I glanced back at him. "Have you heard of personal space?"

"Sorry, after these past few days I just feel closer to you." He put his hands on my shoulders and squeezed, sending those tingles to my lower belly.

I froze, maybe I was just going crazy. Surely, I'd get past my awkward feelings as soon as I got some food in my belly. "Um, you might want to give me some space so I can get my breakfast."

"How about I get you some more coffee?" He snagged my empty cup from my hand as he moved away from me to pour me a fresh cup of joe.

"You must have read my mind." I gave him a small smile before picking up one of the paper plates. Then I set about filling my plate with food.

"What time is it?" I asked glancing at my watch, only the faceplate was shattered, making the time unreadable. Damned expensive pieces of junk.

"Almost nine o'clock," Vlad said as he finished

filling my cup with cream and began stirring in sugar.

"Wow, I did sleep a long time. Huh." It was weird. I really shouldn't have been so tired, and as I thought about it, I could only think of one reason. The power Mara had taken to fuel her little spell. No doubt that was it, but at the same time, I wasn't sure, or at least, I didn't want it to be true because if it was, maybe Mara had done more than she claimed, and the absolute last thing I wanted was for *that* to be true.

"You needed it." Vlad handed me the fresh cup of coffee. "Now enjoy your breakfast because I'm fairly certain you're going to lose your appetite after you hear their plans."

I stared at Vlad for a moment. He was acting a little friendlier than usual. I didn't really do friends, not after I lost my family. We could never be anything more than friends and partners. Not only was it against FBI regulations, I didn't want to take a chance and lose the only true friend I had left in this world. Still, looking at him right now almost made me want more, and that was more concerning than whatever the witches had planned.

14

ALYSON

"Okay, what's going on?" I asked as I poured my third cup of coffee and stirred in milk and sugar.

Vlad pursed his lips. "Let's go into the living room with everyone. It's their plan, let them explain it."

The tension coming off him was palpable. It made me nervous and jittery. He *really* didn't like their plan, and that concerned me. A lot.

"Maybe a third cup was overkill," I mumbled as we walked back into the living room.

"What do you have planned that has Vlad so nervous?" I asked as I took the seat next to Vlad on the window ledge.

Instead of sitting down with me, my partner

stood next to me with his arms crossed and a scowl on his face.

"For the record, while I agree with Vlad, there's no arguing with my mother when she's made up her mind." Stella scowled at her mom.

Well, that was certainly interesting. If both Vlad and Stella agreed, why was Mara still considering it? More importantly, what was she considering?

Mara ignored Stella's scowl as she looked at me. "I want to be used as bait for the terrorists or the werewolves, whoever it is that's after me."

As I stared at the words, I was ashamed to have mixed feelings. Part of me wanted to tell her it was crazy and suicidal, but more of me? More of me wanted to stop the guys killing people. It was a risk, and a bad risk, but at the same time, it was only risking one person, and it might save countless lives if we succeeded.

And this was Mara. While she was a bit kooky, she was definitely powerful. If she thought she could pull this off, I was inclined to at least hear her out.

"Okay." I took a deep breath as Vlad bristled beside me. As he turned his gaze onto me, I continued, "How do you propose to set yourself up as bait? What are you trying to accomplish?"

"They are probably watching our lair," Mara explained. "I think I should go back. I can pretend to be salvaging things. After all, we do have a lot of supplies there. It would make sense to our attackers for me to want to see what survived."

"You think you can go there and they will what? Take you captive and lead us all right to their leader? Really?" I shook my head. "Because I'm one hundred percent sure that plan just leads to you getting sacrificed."

"Their ritual requires time to set up. I've been thinking about it, and even assuming they have all the materials on hand, it'd take a few hours to set up."

"Mara, I think it's great you want to help catch these murderers. I really do, but how do you propose to protect yourself should they capture you? I'm certain they are readier for another ritual then you think." I met her eyes. "Some of the attacks were reported pretty quickly. In those cases, I doubt the whole thing took more than a few minutes." I shook my head. "All they need is a space to perform it, and for all you know, they'll just haul you off to a pre-prepared place."

"I doubt that would work." Mara shook her head. "They would have to find a place where my energy was at home. The best place to do that is my lair and most of it was destroyed. Even if they have everything, it is far from an ideal spot to use, and if they do decide to move me, you can track me. Stella knows how to find me anywhere."

"Hmm, it might work," I was forced to admit. "But if it doesn't, you'll die a horrendous death, *and* they'll be that much closer to their end goal. Do you understand this?"

Mara nodded resolutely. "I know exactly what I'm doing. Don't worry, my mind is clear, and I am ready for this."

The stress of the situation was weighing heavily on the grand witch. She had wrinkles I hadn't seen before. The bags under Mara's eyes showed how tired she was.

"I can't believe we're still talking about using her as bait," Vlad cried, his sudden intrusion into the conversation surprising me. "It's absolutely insane. She could get killed."

"He's right, mom," Stella said before Mara cut her off with a wave of her hand.

"Now listen here both of you." Mara glared at both Vlad and Stella. "I am the great witch and *I* don't need your permission. This is what's happening." She sucked in a breath as she looked to her daughter. "Stella, you need to stay here in case something goes wrong. If you don't hear from me by the end of tomorrow, you will be the coven leader until your sister shows up."

Part of me wanted to argue with her, but I could already see there was no point. Mara was going to do this whether we liked it or not, and she had the spiritual chutzpah to pull it off even if we tried to stop her. Worse, as much as I didn't want to risk letting someone be bait for a bunch of murderous psychopaths, even if she was a witch, her plan just might work. And, right now, we needed something to work. Especially because, if our enemies succeeded it'd bring about the apocalypse.

"Alyson, talk some sense into her," Vlad said, gesturing at Mara. "Make her see reason."

I took a deep breath before turning to look at Mara. "Do you have the strength to do this? Did you get enough sleep? If I agree to this, and I'm not saying I will, you need to be at your best."

"Thank you for your concern, I am fine." Mara nodded resolutely. "That is one thing we will not need to worry about."

"Alyson!" Vlad said, glaring at me, and the look of betrayal on his face made me want to run away.

Only, he was wrong. Mara was a grown woman and her plan was solid, if dangerous. Besides, we'd be there to make sure she was okay, and this was the end of the world.

"You don't look fine, mother." Stella took her mom's hand and patted the back of it.

"Don't worry about me dear. I've lived long enough. Focus on keeping the rest of the coven safe." With that, she stood and looked to me. "Besides, I have a feeling Alyson is more than capable of keeping me safe."

With her words still ringing in my ears, my focus turned to Stella. "Looks like this is happening, so now, it's just a matter of specifics." I ignored Vlad's glare next to me even though I could practically feel it burning into me. "Let's figure out how to keep Mara safe."

15

ALYSON

We made good timing getting to the old witch's lair, but something felt off.

Still, we did have backup. Mara had brought ten guards with her. They all kept looking at each other and back to their great witch like they were all sharing a secret and I was left out.

I looked toward Anita and asked, "Is there something you haven't shared with me?"

"Not that I know of. I think Mara shared all of the details for her plan." Anita, the leader of the guards, gave me a half-smile that didn't quite reach her eyes before flicking her gaze to Mara.

She was definitely hiding something. I just wasn't sure what, and being that this operation involved using Mara as bait, that didn't bode well.

Still, I would protect her as best I could, and if something happened, I'd deal with it then. After all, they may have been witches, but I was a dragon.

We parked a few hundred feet from what once was the main entrance of the industrial park. I got out and looked around, but while I couldn't see anyone, my other senses picked up some seriously wicked vibes. Either the enemy was here or they set a trap for us.

Mara looked at the remains of what had once been her lair. "Be careful, I sense black magic in the air."

The magical bombs they set up really did their job. What had once been a series of six interconnected warehouses and factories was now almost all rubble. Only one warehouse and part of two others still stood.

Anita put her arm around Mara and hugged her. "I don't know how we will recover anything from this."

"Oh, I don't know." Mara gave the other woman a sly smile. "The Goddess gives and the Goddess takes."

"All right, spread out and see what you can find," I ordered. "No one go alone. Stay in pairs. Vlad, you're with me." I didn't care who watched

Mara, I would still have an eye on her. Vlad and I would never get too far from her. Not with so much at stake. Besides, it wasn't like we knew what magical artifacts, if any, would be of value.

When we were far enough away that not even shifter ears could pick me up, I leaned close to Vlad and whispered, "I don't trust her. There's more going on than she has led us to believe. What do you think?"

His lips barely moved as he whispered back, "I agree. While I trust Mara with my life, she is holding something back. When I got up tonight, they were performing spells on each other in the kitchen. They stopped once they heard me."

"Did you ask her about it?" I inquired.

"Yes." He paused for a moment as if mulling over his words. "She said it was none of my business, that it was coven business. She's never kept anything from me before when I asked her."

I leaned down, picking some clothes out of the rubble. We were supposedly here to salvage, I needed to keep up appearances just in case someone was watching.

Vlad was playing along and pulled out a broken vase which he threw on top of another pile of debris. "Anita's right. There won't be much to salvage outside of the one standing building."

"Maybe we can find some vultures to practice throwing junk at," I joked, thinking more about throwing stuff at some evil werewolves when the hair on the back of my neck stood on end. "Vlad?"

He appeared next to me so fast I jumped. "Shh." Vlad gestured toward the still-standing building. "I feel it too. They're here. I'm sure Mara and her guards feel it as well. They are more in tune with anything magical than we are." Vlad waited long enough for me to nod before he headed for the door of the warehouse.

Sensing more than hearing someone approach, I turned around and saw Mara along with all of her guards. She smiled at me as I reached the door.

"Is it okay to open?" When she nodded, I reached for the knob. The second I touched it, dread welled up inside me. Something was definitely wrong in there, and though I wasn't as magically inclined as the witches were, even I could feel it.

Still, standing out here wouldn't help us figure out what was going on. Gritting my teeth, I turned the knob and opened the door.

The smell of fresh blood smashed into my

senses like a bag full of pennies. I staggered backward, one hand going to my nose. Were they in the middle of a ritual? I wasn't sure, but either way it certainly seemed like a possibility. Flames and cauldrons.

As I mulled it over, another thought struck me. Heart racing, I glanced at Vlad, worried his blood lust might take over.

He was edging backward, spine stiff and eyes narrowed in concentration. Still, I could tell it was a losing battle. There was just too much blood. Worse, it was fresh.

"Put the menthol on your lip." I gestured toward the pocket where he kept it. "Then you'll be okay."

With a nod, he pulled the little vial out of his shirt pocket and put a generous portion of menthol on his upper lip, right below his nose. It was so strong, I was able to smell the menthol scent above anything else.

"I'll take point. Have a few of the guards join me and you stay near Mara." I moved ahead and left Vlad to watch over his friend before he could answer me. "No matter what happens, don't let them take her."

If they had already started to sacrifice someone

here they wouldn't need to take Mara anywhere else nor would they need time to set up another ritual. They would just sacrifice her, and the rest of us.

Vlad gave me a pointed look as I drew my Glock. "You be careful. We can't afford to lose you, either."

He had a point. As far as anyone knew, I was the last surviving dragon, but I wasn't planning on letting myself get sacrificed.

As the witches moved to back me up, I moved inside and stepped to the right. My senses were tingling all over, warning me I was stepping into a trap. Worse, as I looked around the dimly lit room, trying to pick out anything that might let me know what was going on my inner voice kept shouting at me to run, far and fast!

One of the witches, Brenda, put her hand on my shoulder and tugged for me to stop.

Turning around to see what she wanted I noticed a glimmer of fear in this warrior's eyes. Did she know what was ahead?

"Wait a second," she said, voice catching as she spoke. "Let me see if I can figure out what they're doing."

"You have ten seconds," I said, shutting my eyes and trying to calm down. My dragon was itching to get out and fight. She wanted to destroy. Normally, she was happy to stay inside and wait for the times when I took her to distant mountaintops and let her fly.

Today, something was agitating her and causing her to want to turn everything and everyone to ash. It must have been the black magic in the air. This case had been messing with all of us since the start.

Since, when in dragon form, bullets just ricocheted off my scales, fire felt good, and it was rare for a sword to penetrate a scale, it made sense for me to take point. Assuming I had enough space, I could shift into a dragon and act as a shield for everyone else.

Of course, I would only do it if our lives were in immediate danger, though. I had no desire to out my secret to anyone else and attract every two-bit hunter from here to Russia. Enough people in this world knew my true form, no one else needed to know, especially a bunch of witches I barely trusted.

"Okay." Brenda's voice startled me, and as I glanced at the witch, she motioned to the left.

I turned at the next intersection. I swear they turned these warehouses into mazes. It was probably a good thing when you lived here, not a good thing when looking for the bad guys. Every corner was a blind spot that could hide a booby trap or bomb.

Stopping at the corner, I put my back against the left wall and looked down the right corridor as far as I could. Then I pulled out a small mirror from my pocket and angled it so I could see what was waiting for us down the left hall.

All I could see was the end of the current corridor. There must have been more turns. Before making a move, I looked above to make sure there wasn't anything in the ceiling waiting for us. I couldn't see any threats but my entire body was screaming, "Danger, danger, Alyson Andrews."

Turning back to the witches behind me, I nodded before making the left turn and heading to the next intersection. They followed me quietly to the next stop. From there, Brenda motioned to the left, and I again checked both ways before moving on. After a few more turns, my fight or flight instincts kicked in so bad, I almost shifted on the spot. We had to be close.

Before I could take another step, Brenda reached out, stopping me. I looked at her questioningly, and she put their fingers to her lips to keep me quiet. I nodded as she reached into her satchel.

She began to count with her fingers, and as she

reached one, she flung the collection of herbs at the wall in front of us. For a moment nothing happen, then the wall was just gone. I stood there, staring openmouthed. There hadn't even been a sound.

Shifting my gaze into the room, I nearly gagged. A dozen unconscious witches were lying beside a bloody pentagram etched into the ground.

The blood-drained bodies of two other witches lay on the outer edges of the circle, making me think they had already been sacrificed because standing in the middle of the pentagram were three massive werewolves and one mammoth of a man. He had a knife in his hand and was draining the life-blood from a witch who was still alive, but barely.

Part of me wanted to rush in, but the scene struck me as odd. There were a set of footprints in the blood that looked too small to belong to the tall man in the center, but larger than a woman's foot, yet I didn't see any other human men in the room. Where was the other person?

I wasn't sure, but as I looked around, I saw a stand with a book and a statue sitting atop it. It was definitely the right shape and size to match the void left behind in our previous crime scenes.

As I shifted my gaze back to the man in the center, the witches with me barged into the room.

A fireball zinged by my ear, slamming into a werewolf, but as the smell of burning hair hit my nose, the creature did little more than look over at us. As it looked down at its chest, one finger going to touch the blackened, burned flesh, I saw it was already starting to heal.

Worse, the others had caught sight of us and were running forward, dodging the witches' projectiles with practiced ease.

As arcs of lightning exploded from Brenda's fingers the wolves broke formation and charged. Part of me wanted to help, but as a witch caught a werewolf with a supercharged roundhouse kick that snapped the thing's neck backward with a thunderclap of force that sent it flying across the room, I realized they probably didn't need it. Besides, I had bigger fish to fry.

Raising my Glock, I fired at the big guy in the center. Only, instead of taking him center mass like they should have, the air in front of him shimmered, causing the bullets to fall lifelessly to the ground.

"Yeah, that's not gonna work, girly," he said, a sinister grin stretching his lips. "Not from there anyway. You'll have to get a lot closer if you want to shoot me." He gestured at me with the knife. It had a bejeweled handle but the blade looked to be rusting at the hilt. Still, I could tell the weapon was ancient and filled with a type of dark magic. Either way, dragon or not, I really didn't want to get cut by it.

"Yeah, I can do that," I growled, holstering my gun. The crazy thing was, I wanted to do it. My inner dragon screamed for me to rush at him, for me to tear into him with my bear hands.

"Excellent." He took a step toward me as I unsheathed the short sword I had strapped to my right leg.

His eyes widened is surprise as I rushed through the melee toward him. Unfortunately, he recovered from his shock by the time I reached him, and as I got near enough to attack, he lashed out at me with the knife in his hand.

I deflected his strike with my sword as I pulled the gun from my belt and shot him. While this time the bullet hit him, it still barely seemed to affect him. He didn't even stagger backward. Instead, he thrust his knife at me.

I sidestepped his next thrust, getting a too-close look at that knife as it went past my face.

"What's the matter, upset your little trick didn't work?" the man asked as his knee shot out, catching me in the stomach and driving me back a couple steps. "Honestly, I expected more from the FBI." He shook his head. "You'll barely be a fitting sacrifice."

"Buddy, I haven't even started trying to kick your butt," I said, shrugging off his blow. It hadn't been that strong, but it had caught me by surprise. "And I won't be needing this to do it." I sheathed my sword and raised my fists.

As he began to laugh, my dragon's might filled me. "You expect to fight me unarmed—"

I interrupted him by driving my fist into his stomach. The blow knocked him backward a few steps, and as he bent over to try and regain his balance, he stumbled over the woman he had been sacrificing.

She cried out in pain as the man toppled over crashing into the stand and knocking the statue and book to the ground.

The man shook himself, trying to regain himself as I moved to the woman.

"Come on," I said, grabbing her arm, and as I went to pull her to her feet, the guy tackled me. We slammed into the ground hard and my head cracked against the stone floor. As my vision went dark around the edges, he reared back to hit me.

As I tried to raise my arms to defend myself, his fist crashed into my chin. Stars shot across my eyes and pain shot through me. The taste of blood filled my mouth as he struck again. This time I caught his fist.

His eyes widened as I bore down with all my strength, and the bones in his hand creaked painfully. A scream tore from his lips, but that didn't stop him from trying to hit me with his other hand. Only as he raised his fist, the witch I'd saved came up behind him with the statue from the stand in both hands. With a desperate swing, she slammed it into the back of his skull.

He roared in pain as he collapsed to the ground beside me. This time, I wasted no time, leaping atop him and pinning him down.

"It's over," I cried, and as the words left my lips he began to laugh.

"You can't stop us! We are many and more are waiting to be called." Then, before I could ask him about his special brand of crazy, he burst into flames. The smell of charred meat hit my nose, and if I'd been anyone other than me, I'd have caught on fire. Fortunately, I was me, and so while the fire was annoying, I managed to get off of him without getting immolated.

"How did you survive that?" the witch asked, staring at me in confusion.

"FBI magic." I nodded to her before turning to the rest of the battle. While one of the werewolves was lying on the ground, dead, three more were still engaged in battle with the witches.

"I need one of them alive," I yelled out. "If I can interrogate one, maybe we could figure this out."

Brenda nodded to me right before thick black smoke erupted from her fingers. It hit the charging wolf full in the face, and as his hands went to his eyes, she drove her knife into his right forepaw. A blood curdling scream erupted from his lips as he fell to the ground, screaming and whimpering far out of proportion to the damage he'd taken.

"There's your one." Brenda snorted, before turning to help her sisters-at-arms, and shouting something in Latin.

"What did you do?" I asked as I rushed over to wrangle the wounded wolf.

"I cast a pain spell that increases pain by one hundred fold. Hurry, help me to tie him up." Brenda pulled some rope from her pack.

Nodding, I hopped on top of the writhing beast, but even with my enhanced strength, it was hard to keep it pinned. "Stop fighting," I growled right before I drove my elbow into his chest.

The earsplitting howl that burst from the werewolf nearly shattered my hearing, but it made it a lot easier to hold him down. Man, I really needed a spell like this. "Why don't you use this spell every time you fight? Seems like it would help turn the tides in your favor."

"It takes too much of my energy to wield it. I only use it when I need a prisoner, otherwise, I just try to kill our enemies," Brenda reasoned as she uncoiled the thick rope.

There was an explosion to the left, and as I glanced toward it, I saw the two remaining wolves had been flung through the block wall. Sparks leapt from their skin as they struggled to rise, but before they could, the witches rushed in, swords raised. It was over before I even turned my attention back to the wolf beneath me.

"Help us to keep this one from running," I called from atop the beast.

"On it," the left witch said, hand splayed toward me. Green light exploded from her fingers moments before emerald chains erupted from the ground, wrapping around the wolf and holding it down. Even still, I could tell the binding wouldn't last long, but then again we didn't need long.

Taking advantage of the situation, Brenda quickly finished tying up the beast, and the second she was done I got right into his snout and began my interrogation. "Who are you?"

"It doesn't matter," he snarled. "You won't be able to stop us. This world will be cleansed and you will not survive."

"Neither will you if you open the veil between Hell and Earth," I countered. Was this guy serious? "Those demons won't let you live. They will destroy the entire planet. It will literally be Hell on Earth. Why would you want to let them out? It's suicide!"

Instead of replying, he snapped at me. His fangs passed within inches of my neck, but I was way too fast for him to catch me given our current positions.

"Oh no, that won't do," Brenda chided right before she threw a handful of herbs onto the werewolf. Another scream tore from the beast as his body pulled itself back into human form against its will. Just watching it made me feel bad.

"What did you do to me?" he asked, looking around wide-eyed before fixing his gaze on the witch.

"Making you more willing to answer our questions." She smirked. "Go ahead, Alyson. Ask away. You'll find him much more inclined to answer."

"This is why we fight." He spat at her.

"That doesn't matter." I smacked him just hard enough to get his attention back onto me. "Why are you letting the demons out?"

"Nothing you do to me will matter." He began to laugh. "Once the demons come, they will help us destroy all who do not join us."

"They won't be controlled by werewolves. Surely you must realize this!"

"We already control them." He was nuts. The power must have done something to his brain.

"Who's in charge? Who's telling you what to do?"

"You will never get close to our leader. There are hundreds of us protecting him."

"Where are they? If he has so much protection, surely it won't matter if you tell us his location." I hoped he'd fall for it but doubted he would.

"You don't deserve to be in his presence. You might as well go home and enjoy your last days on Earth." He spit at me.

I narrowed my eyes at him, partially because getting spit on always pissed me off, and partially because there was no way in hell I was letting a guy like this start the apocalypse. "Answer the question. Tell me where to find—"

Before I could finish, I heard screaming off in the distance followed by Vlad yelling for my help.

16

ALYSON

"See if you can get any more info out of him," I said, leaping to my feet and heading back the way we'd come. While I wasn't sure what had caused Vlad to call for me, I knew it must be bad. He wouldn't have done it otherwise. That almost made it worse because it meant he was in trouble, and the idea of him getting hurt scared me a lot more than I'd expected.

My chest heaved with effort as I reached the exit and stepped outside. Vlad and the six witch warriors protecting Mara were fighting a losing battle against a dozen werewolves. There was no way they could beat all of them. Worse, two witches were already down and only one werewolf was injured.

"Mara, use that magic of yours!" I screamed as

I pulled out my sword and raced forward. While I wanted to use my Glock, I couldn't risk shooting any of my allies.

"I am! These wolves have somehow found a way to counter-act my magic! It's not working," the great witch screamed as she threw a spell at a nearby wolf like she was trying to illustrate her point.

Light blue electrical arcs ripped across the shifter's body, knocking him flat on his back. Only, by the time I'd made it to Mara, he was back on his feet. His claws raked out, slashing against Mara's shield, and that's when I realized the problem. Everyone else was inside Mara's shield.

As the werewolf sprang at me, claws raised, I shifted into my dragon form without thinking. The world seemed to stop for a handful of seconds as everyone paused and just stared open-mouthed.

I doubted any of them except for Vlad had seen a dragon before, but that was fine. I could use this too my advantage. While they were still shocked, I let my fire-filled scream erupt. The blast caught the leaping werewolf full on, reducing him to a pile of ash in the blink of an eye.

The rest of the werewolves took one look at the handful of ash that remained of their companion before taking off. Ignoring the witches who were safe behind Mara's shield, I heaved another blast of flame at them.

My dragon fire caught another, reducing the top half of his body to cinders. That's when two of his buddies tried to take advantage of his death by leaping at me. I spun, smashing the first with my tail. His body exploded like a bag full of raspberry jam.

My forearm caught the second one in the chest, knocking him into the far wall with enough force to reduce him to a smear.

Unfortunately, while the two of them had attacked me, the rest had continued running, and part of me wondered if they'd sacrificed themselves so their friends could get away. Either way, it didn't matter. I wasn't letting them escape now that they'd seen me.

My wings unfurled and I tried to get into the air, but the warehouse was too small for me to fly around in. I barely had enough room for my head. Standing at full height, I was almost twenty feet high and my wingspan was double my height.

The majority of the wolves were trying to get to the back of the warehouse where an emergency exit stood. They weren't going to get away so easily.

I charged toward them while sucking in another chest full of air and let it rip. My fire consumed everything in my path, including the remaining werewolves. Unfortunately, as my flame washed over the emergency exit, I realized this building wasn't going to survive my fire, either.

Dragon fire was far deadlier than a normal fire. The more oxygen I took in, and the greater my rage, the closer I could get to spitting out a purple flame, the hottest, brightest flame I had ever produced. It was rare, but I had done it before. So far, my inferno was orange with a few white tipped flames, but that was still more than enough to devour nearly everything in its path.

In front of me, everything I could see was up in flames, my flames. The emergency exit door was covered in a firestorm. My fire licked up the paint covering the metal door before starting to scorch and melt it. No one was going to leave that way.

I turned to find Vlad and Mara were the only ones left in the room. Vlad had a frown on his face while Mara's eyes were open wide in astonishment.

"We got everyone out," Vlad said in a voice that told me he was trying to make the best of the situation. "You saved a lot of lives, Alyson."

Smoke blew out my nose as I tried to calm

down and make sure I didn't burn up the remaining exit. "Sorry about the place," I grunted in a deep, guttural voice.

Mara finally seemed to recover. "Don't worry about it. I'm just glad you killed all of them before they could leave. We have a lot of injured to take back to our safe house. Can you switch back to your human form and help us?"

Vlad spoke up for me, "She has to stay in this form for a while. Since she doesn't shift often enough, when she does take her dragon form, she needs to stay in it for at least an hour."

"Oh." Mara bit her lip, thinking as she scanned the warehouse. "Where is Brenda?"

"Back that way," I pointed to the far end of the warehouse. The flames hadn't reached that far yet, but they would given enough time.

"I'll go get them," Vlad said before gesturing outside. "Alyson, two werewolves got out behind us. Why don't you scour the area and see if you can find them?"

I nodded in reply, careful as I turned around to not hit them with my fifteen-foot tail. It was extremely dangerous for me to shift while in the confines of a warehouse given the small confines.

One wrong move and I could accidentally crush one of my friends.

Dragons just weren't meant to be indoors. We were designed to roam the skies and live in gigantic caves on the tops of mountains most people wouldn't dare climb.

As soon as I sensed that Vlad and all the witches were safely away from the building, I barreled through the blazing wall and out into the open night.

I took to the skies as soon as I was clear and looked for any signs of the werewolves. I couldn't let them get away. They knew my secret. Once they shared it, I would be on everyone's hit list. My identity would no longer be a secret. My life would be in more danger than it ever had, especially if *he* ever found out.

17

VLAD

"Mara, please know I'm truly sorry we were unable to get there in time to save everyone," I said as we reached the safe house in Compton. "However, Alyson just sacrificed herself to save you. You must swear an oath that you and your coven will die protecting her secret. If anyone finds out she's the last living dragon, her life will be over."

I still couldn't believe Alyson shifted in front of everyone to save Mara. She didn't even like Mara. I was absolutely grateful for her sacrifice but scared as well. The secret was out.

There was always a group of hunters who wanted to find dragons. Something about dragon scales having immense power and making the best flak jackets. Bullets couldn't penetrate dragon scales, after all. That was aside from the general shifter power struggle. Dragons were naturally at the top, but since they'd been gone for so long, other groups were vying for power. Should they find out dragons still existed, those still in charge would seek to take Alyson down just to cement their place in the hierarchy.

"Don't worry, Vlad." Mara met my eyes, and the depth of understanding I saw in her eyes surprised me. "Alyson is now a part of our coven, just like you. We protect our own and never share their secrets, not even with other covens. Alyson saved over a dozen witches today. Trust me. Her secret is safe." Mara bowed her head, a sign of true respect from a great witch.

I didn't doubt this coven would go to their graves keeping Alyson's secret, especially after she'd saved them. Witches were particular like that.

No. The hard part would be making Alyson understand that. It wouldn't be easy. When I first found out she was a dragon, she'd almost killed me on the spot. That was also when I'd been assigned to be her partner. Our Section Chief figured if I was her partner, then she would accept I not only knew the truth, but with my mind-altering abilities could help her keep her secret.

Still, I couldn't erase the memories of the were-wolves who got away. It made me hope she would find the fleeing werewolves and fry them all. She'd feel better if she did. Then maybe she'd listen to reason.

"How are the women we rescued from the ritual? Do they know anything about what's going on and who's behind it?" They had been captured and held for at least a day, maybe longer, so who knew what they might have gleaned.

"They will be fine. My witches will heal with some rest and a little nourishment. They did over-hear some of what's going on, namely that those eco-terrorists are working with the werewolves."

"So it's like we suspected. Now we know for sure." I nodded once. "I'm going to try and call this in to command. Hopefully, the phones are working now."

I left Mara alone while I went to the kitchen to make the call. The sun would be up soon, and while I needed to sleep, this call was important. The FBI needed all the pieces to this case, and we needed more help.

Unfortunately, like before, the call just rang and rang. Not even a voicemail picked up. Tomorrow, we'd need to make a trip to command.

We needed more firepower, more men, especially since magic wasn't working like it should. After all, if we couldn't blast them with magic, a few M-16 bullets would put them down.

Annoyed, I walked back into the living room where Mara sat with her daughter, Stella.

Her brow was furrowed and she was hugging her mother. "Mom, are you sure you're all right? Using so much magic these past two days has to have drained you."

"I'm fine, dear," Mara tutted. "I just need some rest, like everyone else. Will you stay up and wait for Alyson to return?"

"Yes, of course." Stella looked up to me and smiled. "Do you think she'll want anything in particular? After all she did to save us, it's the least we can do."

"She's going to be in a rotten mood when she gets here, so I doubt it much matters." I shrugged. "Maybe I should try staying awake until she returns?"

"No, you go ahead and sleep, Vlad." Mara stood up to leave but stopped before she exited the room. "Stella, be sure to wake me up when Alyson arrives. I need to speak with her before she does anything rash." With that, Mara turned down a hall and went to her room.

As the sun was getting ready to show itself on the horizon, I went to go lay down with a heavy heart. It might be best if Alyson found somewhere else to sleep today and joined back up with us tonight, when she'd had some time to cool down. Too bad I couldn't call her and suggest it.

18

ALYSON

I circled the area surrounding the lair, looking for the wolves who got away, but after a few dozen passes, I realized it was hopeless. They'd probably shifted back to human form.

Even though the witches had lived in an industrial complex, it wasn't far from civilization, and if they'd reverted, I wouldn't be able to pick them out. Sure, I could kill everyone I saw in the hopes I found them, but the last thing I needed was to have more blood on my hands.

As soon as I realized I wasn't going to find them without outing myself to others, I had two choices: I could stress over the situation and make myself sick or I could choose to enjoy my time. Since I had zero control over it at this point, I chose to do the latter.

I turned and flew into the Angeles National

Forest. It had been way too long since my last shift. The thrill of flying was something I had truly missed. So, I flew around the areas I knew weren't inhabited. The scent of pine and fresh air combined to make an aroma better than any scented candle I had ever owned. My wings spread out and I soared through the night sky reveling in the freedom, even if it was for only a couple of hours.

As the sun started to peak over the horizon, I flew down as far as I thought I could safely get before stopping and descending into the tree line. There, I turned back to my human form and pulled my cellphone from my pocket. Thank God that, through some magic I didn't fully understand, my clothing and anything else I was wearing disappeared when I shifted instead of being destroyed or ripped to shreds.

Unfortunately, just because my cellphone had survived, didn't mean it still worked. While the battery indicator showed only five percent left, there was no cell coverage where I was anyway. All I could do was head toward the highway and hope to catch a ride back to Compton. I should have made sure Vlad left me a car somewhere.

Four hours, three different rides, and a bus later,

I finally made it back to the witch's safe house. I was exhausted but still ticked off. I didn't know if I could trust the coven to keep my secret, but I hoped they would.

I couldn't even think about those two werewolves. My best chance was that they didn't know exactly who I was or, even better, they died on their way back to whoever they reported to. Since my luck seemed to have run out a few days back, I doubted I would be so lucky.

Stella was the only one still up when I arrived.

"Alyson!" She kept her distance as she spoke. "Thank you for saving my family. I don't know how to repay you for what you've done."

"You're welcome." I tried to smile because that was what people were supposed to do when they were thanked, but all I could think about was that my secret was out and my days were numbered. "Where is everyone?"

Stella rattled off her words in a formal and distant manner, like she was afraid of me. "Asleep. It was an exhausting night. I stayed up waiting for you. My mother wanted me to wake her when you arrived. Please, let me get her so you two can talk." She gave me a tiny smile as she went to wake her mother. "We will be keeping your secret, by the way. You have nothing to worry about."

The next few minutes passed with mind-numbing slowness. All I could think about was my secret. Sure, Stella had said they'd keep it, but at the same time, she hadn't even been there. Clearly, Mara had told her, and if she'd told Stella, who else had she told?

As I let the questions rattle around in my head, I found myself staring at pictures of Mara with her family. Those brought me thoughts of my own family. I felt a stab of remorse as the memory of their deaths hit me.

I hadn't been there to help protect them when they'd been murdered. Worse, I didn't even know who killed them, just that we had been tracked for years by someone wanting our scales. Dad had said it was hunters. Mom had another theory. She thought the evidence pointed to witches.

They had sent me to a school for humans, insisting it was important I learn how to fit in with them so I could hide in plain sight. That was the only reason I'd survived. I had been away at a weekend camp with my classmates when it happened, and the mystery of their death still haunted me. Part of it was survivor's guilt, sure, but mostly? Mostly, I just wanted revenge.

Still, up until now, I'd come up empty. Hell, even with my pull in the FBI, I had no real clue as to who had killed them. The only thing the old case files said was that there were signs magic had been used. Between that and my mother's suspicions, I had always assumed witches were somehow involved. While that wasn't enough to make me hate witches, per se, that combined with what I'd seen rogue witches do to the unwary, and the possibility that one could sense what I was, made it so I didn't trust them. At all.

"Alyson! Thank goodness you're all right! Did you get the other werewolves?" Mara was still in her dressing gown as she rushed in. She hadn't even taken the time to change into appropriate clothes. She had on a pink flowery nightgown which flowed down to her ankles. Her hair was disheveled and her eyes weren't even fully opened yet. She reminded me of my grandma, and somehow, that hurt as much as it helped.

"Mara. I'm glad you're all right. How's the woman I saved from the sacrifice? Will she make it?" I hoped my shifting at least saved that woman from a horrific death.

"Yes, she'll be fine. Thank you so much for everything you have done. I know Vlad wanted to speak with you when you arrived, but he is already asleep. I wanted to have some time to speak with you before everyone else woke up. Would you like some breakfast?"

"Yeah, I could use some food and coffee, please." My stomach rumbled, and as I looked down at it, Mara laughed.

"Well, come along then. I'll fix us something."

Stella seemed to recognize that as her cue to depart. "Mother, I'm going to sleep now. Alyson, thank you again."

"You're welcome." I nodded to her as Mara and I headed into the kitchen.

"First, I want to make sure you know none of us will share this secret," Mara said, moving toward the coffee pot as she spoke. "I told Stella because she may need to lead our coven if her sisters aren't at the other safe house." She seemed to deflate a touch as she turned on the pot. "None of the witches we rescued have seen them."

"Do they know what happened to everyone else?" I asked, suddenly feeling bad for worrying about myself. This woman's family was missing, and here I was being selfish.

Still, if the werewolves had her daughters, I would have expected them to be in the warehouse where we found the others. It made the most sense since the sacrifice had to take place somewhere they called home. Therefore, the warehouse was the logical destination for all the witches they wanted to sacrifice from this coven.

"No, they split up when they got attacked. My daughters and some of the sentinels took the children from our coven and tried to get away. Keeping the children safe was the most important thing. The women we found at the old lair were the ones who volunteered to stay behind to give the others time to get away." The sigh coming from Mara was enough to tell me she feared the worst.

Shoot, I did too. "With the phones down, there's no way to know if they made it safely?"

"We have a way to attempt communication but I need all of my coven members who are here to help me. It will take an enormous amount of power to reach out telepathically to my daughters, especially if one of them didn't make it."

"I'm sorry you don't know if they're safe. I truly hope they are." Strangely, it was true. Even though they were witches, I really did hope they were okay.

"Thank you, dear. It means a lot to me. I hope

you can trust me when I say my entire coven has now adopted you. By saving the lives of those who were about to be offered up as a sacrifice to the demons, you have become one of us."

"Oh, um. Thanks?" I shifted uncomfortably. Normally, I would have stormed out and not looked back, but this coven was different from any other witches I had encountered.

Maybe, just maybe, we could become allies. I didn't want to say friends, only because I really had one friend, Vlad. Trust wasn't something I gave very easily. It had to be earned, and it took an awful lot to earn my trust.

"So," I continued, "does this mean every single one of your coven members will take my secret with them to the grave?" I had to know for sure, regardless of whether those two werewolves ratted me out. It was a matter of trust now.

"Yes, it does. Think of us as the witch version of the FBI, our secrets are top secret, compartmentalized. No one will say a word. In fact, we won't even discuss it."

If I could trust her, then this could work for me. If not, well, I didn't want to think about *that* scenario. I considered what she said and decided I didn't have much choice but to trust them. "All right, for now, I trust my secret is safe." I sighed, looking at my shoes. "I do have another question though."

"What's that, dear?" Mara turned to offer me a cup of coffee full of cream and sugar, which I greedily accepted. "Ask away."

"How do you know Vlad so well?" I felt ridiculous asking, but Vlad had insinuated they were a couple at one time. Knowing Vlad, it would be like pulling teeth to get it out of him. So, if possible, I wanted to get the truth from Mara.

Mara had a dreamy expression as she sipped her coffee. She let out a soft sigh. "Vlad was the lover of my youth. We first met in early 1971. My parents let me date him for over a year before they told me it was time to grow up and put away my fantasies. I believe they thought I would naturally move on from him if they let me continue seeing him and when I didn't, they found me a husband."

"You had an arranged marriage? Really?" I scrunched my nose in disdain for the antiquated ritual. Women should be able to choose their own husbands.

Mara shrugged. "Things were different back then for the paranormal. It was imperative I marry another witch who would solidify the blood lines and provide heirs to take over one day when I die."

"I don't know how you can be so cavalier about being forced to marry someone you don't love. I couldn't do it." I shook my head.

"Even if it meant the possibility of bringing your species back from extinction?" She raised an eyebrow at me.

I thought about it a minute. "I guess if there was only one male dragon left, it would be my duty to mate with him. From what I've heard, I'm either the last of my kind or if not, there are very few others. If the latter, I still might be able to choose who I want."

"Maybe, but there are many reasons why you might have to accept a proposal from someone you don't love." Mara took another sip of coffee, seeming to relish it. "I'm very happy I married Logan. He was a good man and a great father. My girls adored him and he thought the sun and moon revolved around them."

"So, you fell in love with him over time?" To be honest, though I'd heard of that happening, it still shocked me.

"Yes, and he with me. We had a wonderful marriage until the werewolves killed him." She waved a hand. "But, I doubt you wanted to know about my husband and children. Was there anything else you wanted to ask about?"

Mara was lucky, she could say she had two loves during her time here on Earth. I doubt I'd trust anyone enough to fall in love once, let alone twice.

"No," I took a long drink of coffee and looked at the ceiling. Part of me wanted to ask her about my parents, but what if she felt attacked by my questions, or worse, was somehow involved?

"Alyson, are you sure? You look like you have a question but are afraid to ask. You may ask me anything." The great witch sat there with a small smile on her face. It was almost as though she already knew what I was going to ask.

"Actually, there is something." I chewed on my words for a moment. "When my entire family was murdered, I was away at a school event. No one knows for sure what happened to my parents or the rest of my tribe. The only thing I know for sure is magic was involved in their death."

My family were some of the last dragons on Earth, which is why my parents wanted me to try fitting in so badly with humans. If everyone thought I was human, I would be safe.

I took a deep breath before continuing. "Do you

happen to know anything about the end of the dragons? Who was chasing us and killed off my entire species?"

Mara put her hand on mine. "Dear, just because magic was used doesn't mean it was witches. We have just witnessed a sinister breed of werewolves with magical abilities."

That was true. This day had certainly thrown all my preconceived notions awry. Still, I'd spent quite a bit of time studying magic, and while I'd never learned any myself, everything pointed to witches being the only ones strong enough to kill my parents. After all, while run of the mill hunters might be a threat to a lone dragon or maybe even a pair, it would be hard for them to eradicate an entire species over a few years' time.

"Yeah, I know, it's just…" I trailed off, unsure of how to continue.

"I suppose now is as good a time as any." Mara sighed. "I was going to wait to speak of this once Vlad was awake, but since it might concern you directly, I may as well tell you now. One of the women you helped rescue, Daisy, told me their captors were part of a secretive order of were-wolves called the Shadow Walkers. They have the ability to use magic but not like we do. Their magic is dark, a power that comes from worshiping demons."

"Wait, I thought no one outside of witches or halflings could use magic? I mean sure, dragons and fae too, but I've never even heard of demons being real." I shook my head.

What she said, didn't make sense. At least, as far as I'd seen. What's more, this was getting complicated. It flew in the face of what I knew about paranormals and magic. Could it be possible there are other creatures out there able to handle magic? If so, could demons have been used to kill my family. I wasn't sure, but the urge to pull the cold case files and show them to Mara was so overwhelming, I almost couldn't think past it.

"Why do you think the dragons have been destroyed?" Mara's question to my question made me feel we were about to go down the rabbit hole again.

"What does that have to do with witches or witchy werewolves or whatever it is we're dealing with?" I sighed, trying to get back on track. Worrying about what happened to my kind right now wouldn't help with the apocalypse. "I'm sorry, can you just start at the beginning?"

"You're not understanding." She watched me

for a long moment, clearly thinking. "Didn't you know you have magic? It has to be honed and practiced, but all dragons are born with an innate gift of magic."

"I did know that, but my parents were killed before they had any chance to teach me how we dragons performed magic, and it wasn't like I had anyone else to ask." I shrugged. "I can sense magic, can practically taste it in the air. Now, I haven't had much experience with witches, but did you know that your magic has more of an earthy taste than an ashy one? Growing up, my parents had witch friends who came over. Whenever they left, I tasted ash. The electrical charge is similar, though yours is stronger, but that's to be expected from a great witch and her daughters, right?"

"Alyson, that's my point exactly." Mara put her coffee mug down. "Each species with magical abilities has a different taste to their power. We all put off an electrical field, but the scent or flavor of our magic is different. Yours come from elemental magic like mine, but it's a different element."

"Hold up, you're saying I have elemental magic?" I scrunched up my nose, thinking.

I had never even heard the term elemental magic before, but then again, most of what the FBI knew about the supernatural was classified, and what wasn't could fit in a thimble. That, combined with my worry over a witch finding me out, made it so I'd never really gleaned the deeper aspects of the craft. Still, I obviously knew what the elements were, and I'd read some fiction books that talked about elemental magic, but I'd thought that had just been fiction. Clearly I'd been wrong.

"Yes, dear." Mara smiled softly. "Now, can you guess what element I might be?"

"Oh!" I thought again of the earthy taste in my mouth. "A witch is of the earth element, right? So, I guess my element is probably fire since dragons breathe fire?" Now that I thought about it, the whole elemental magic thing was actually starting to make sense, though I wasn't sure how I felt about that.

"Exactly. There are also water and air elementals. All of our magic comes from the Earth. It was never designed to harm, but to help. Unfortunately, not everyone uses their powers responsibly, not even humans."

I took another sip of my coffee, which was getting cold from sitting so long. "The werewolves I faced had a different feel, though. It's evil for sure, but there's something else to it. Do you know why?"

"Yes, I believe I do. Anyone can choose the dark side, and these wolves have done more than choose it, they have embraced it and let themselves be over-taken with it."

She sounded like the small green guy from one of my favorite movies as she continued, "The power of good and the power of evil. It's a choice. Although, should a non-magical creature give themselves over to the dark, they become consumed by evil and gain power in exchange. Usually, this power comes from demons."

Mara was blowing my world view. Nothing was as I thought if this witch could be believed. "Are you going to try telling me again God is real? The Devil and his minions are behind this threat? Demons are one thing, I can sort of get behind that, but the Big D? That seems a touch... crazy."

"Yes, I am. I thought you understood that the other day when we discussed the apocalypse?" She gave me a confused look.

At the time, it had been easier to let Mara think I was onboard with her thought process than to disagree. Now though, now I was considering it, and that was ten kinds of crazy.

"Seriously? I thought the whole Heaven and

Hell thing was something our parents told us as kids to make sure we turned out good."

When I first learned of this spell, I thought maybe it was something to bring over another type of power from an alternate dimension. I didn't really believe demons would be raised from Hell. An alternate dimension made more sense.

"You don't think it could be another dimension? These werewolves could be trying to collide our universe with another. What we think of as demons could just be another form of paranormal creature in a multiverse." This was something I actually thought about over the years. I had believed in the multi-verse theory ever since I'd joined the FBI.

"Dear, you watch too much TV. The only other dimensions are Heaven and Hell. The multiverse is just a theory scientists made up. They can't prove it or disprove it." Mara shook her head.

"I guess but I think it makes more sense." I crossed my arms over my chest.

Mara kept that soft, thoughtful smile. "All right, let's just assume there really is a Heaven and a Hell for the moment, whether alone or part of a multi-verse. From everything you have heard, would allowing the demons free reign here be good?"

"No, it would end the world." I sighed. "We're definitely in agreement on that."

"And if your multiverse theory was correct? Would allowing two universes to collide be a good thing for us?" Mara made it sound so simple.

"I see your point. It would also end our world as we know it. Either way, the world will end." No matter what my religious beliefs were, I couldn't allow this spell to be cast.

"Exactly, so let's get back on topic, please." Mara did have a point there.

"Right, magic." I rubbed my face. "So, back to what you were saying, if I understand you properly, elemental magic is inherently good. If that's the case, any other magic should be evil. It would be the balancing effort of the universe, right?"

"With a few small exceptions, you are correct." Mara nodded.

"What do we do about it? Are there other magic wielders we can call? Those who use air or water? Can they help?" I didn't know of any, but Mara might.

"If we had phones. It might be possible or you could go back to your base and ask your boss if he has a way to contact them. I would imagine the FBI knows about their existence and how to reach them." She chuckled. "There might even be an ambassador."

Something about the way she spoke made me think Mara knew more about my agency than I did. Ambassadors? Was it possible? If it was, had my parents been in contact with FBI ambassadors?

No. Those were questions for another day. What mattered now was stopping this ritual. My time with Mara had answered a lot of the questions I'd had over the years, but it'd also opened up so many more.

Was there more to my powers than I knew? If so, how would I learn to use them if there were no more dragons to teach me? Most importantly, how could I use my magic to stop the coming apocalypse?

19

ALYSON

"Mara, I'm going to try calling base again. Someone at command needs to know what's going on." If we didn't stop the Shadow Walkers soon, there would be nothing left to save.

That said, part of the reason I wanted to make the call was so I could have a few minutes to process. So, under the guise of making the call, I went to the garage for some peace and quiet.

This was an awful lot to take in. Demons were real. Hell was real. How could my parents not tell me everything? I was only fifteen at the time, sure, but they also knew someone was coming for us. They should have warned me somehow, left me a notebook full of our secrets, or something.

Instead, I was all alone, forced to work with

witches who may or may not be responsible for destroying my species. Then again, maybe it wasn't witches who were responsible after all. Maybe it was these shadow wolves who tried to kill my people off? Flames and cauldrons, how could there even be shadow wolves? How was that even a thing? Worse, how did I not know about them? How much more didn't I know?

I wasn't sure, but whining about my lack of knowledge wouldn't help things. No, doing something would, if only to keep my mind off the hellish shadow wolves. It was time to reach out to headquarters.

I dialed the number I knew by heart and waited as it rang and rang. Taking a deep breath, I realized that if the phones were down, I should never have received a signal to begin with.

Stupid Alyson! Why didn't you think of this sooner?

Running back into the kitchen, I caught Mara right before she left the room. "Mara, why is the phone ringing but nothing is going through? If the phones are still down, shouldn't I have gotten nothing at all?"

"If all phones services were down, yes, but as I understood it, they were slowly getting services back on. So, it's not surprising it would ring but not actually go through." She yawned. "It's been a long day. I think I need some beauty rest." She gave me a weary smile. "Maybe you should get some rest too."

"Yeah, okay. I will in a minute." I was tired and my brain may not have been firing on all cylinders, but something was causing the tingles, which usually meant something wasn't right in the state of Denmark.

It had been several days since our terrorists/werewolves knocked down our telephone services, including some key cell towers, and while I knew the FBI would be all over it, someone should have returned my emails by now. That someone hadn't was worrying to say the least.

Opening my phone again, I checked for the bars to signal some cell service, and when I once again saw nothing, I wished I had my satellite phone once again. Still, it was strange. I shouldn't have been able to call at all if there were no bars.

Looking around the room, I found a landline. It was one thing to hear ringing when dialing on a cell, but a dial tone on a land line was something totally different. Cell phones didn't have a dial tone. Landlines did. I lifted the handset expecting to hear nothing. Instead, I heard the dial tone all landlines had.

"Why does the landline have a dial tone? Will it work?" I mused aloud as I proceeded to dial the FBI again. It rang and rang without any type of pick up. No message, no recorder, no person picked up. It made me wonder what would happen if I used the satellite phone. Would the same thing happen? Hell, was that why my email wasn't working? Maybe it wasn't getting through either.

I hung up the phone and picked it back up. Trying something new, I dialed my own cell phone. On the landline, I could hear it ringing but there was no ringing from my cellphone. The lines really were still down. It was just strange I was getting dial tones but nothing was going through. Maybe Mara was right, they were just in the middle of fixing everything and those tones were only the first step.

Sleep was what I needed so I went to my room to lay down.

I WOKE up after the sun had set because I shared a biological clock with a vampire of all things. The house was fairly quiet, but I could hear some indistinct talking out beyond my room.

My stomach rumbled, but I definitely needed a shower and some new clothes, otherwise I was going to lose my mind. I still hadn't changed clothes nor showered for days even though I'd been in battles and had been traipsing around bloody crime scenes and whatnot. Sure, a little three day old dried blood never hurt anyone, but I didn't want to wear it anymore.

It made me wish I'd gone home instead of to this safe house, but doing so might leave the witches vulnerable to attack, and with everything that had happened, that didn't seem like a good idea in the slightest. Besides, if someone's home was going to get attacked, it might as well be theirs.

Making my way out, I bumped into Vlad as he exited the bathroom. He had a towel wrapped around his waist, revealing a well-sculpted muscular chest that I tried very hard not to look at because , well, it did certain things to my body that had me think about jumping him again.

"Sorry, I'm just finishing up." He gave me a smile that made me flush for reasons I couldn't quite admit. "Stella had some new clothes brought in for us." He turned, causing the towel to slip down a couple precarious inches. Lower, part of me cried.

He turned back to me. "They are on the counter in there. I grabbed the duffel with your stuff by accident." He shot me another smile. "Now if you'll excuse me." He marched his mostly naked ass past me and into the living room.

"Oh, Vlad!" I heard one of the girls call as I shook my head. I wasn't sure why this attraction was happening now, just that I had to squash it down for good.

Taking a deep breath, I moved into the bathroom and found a duffel bag on the counter just like he'd said. Inside was a toothbrush, deodorant, a hairbrush, as well as an off the rack navy suit similar to the one I'd been wearing.

Part of me was annoyed, but most of me? Most of me was happy as a puppy in a field of wildflowers. Shutting the door, I stripped down to my birthday suit and looked at myself. I didn't' have any scrapes or bruises from the fight thanks to my accelerated healing, but I looked tired on a bodily level.

"Guess it can't be helped," I muttered, moving to the shower and turning on the hot water. As soon as it reached maximum temperature, I stepped in and tried to enjoy the spray. Only, my stomach kept rumbling, so instead of relaxing I just got sort of hangry. I grabbed the sealed hotel-sized soaps and shampoo off the rack in the shower and set to work.

Fifteen minutes later, I felt almost human, or as human as I could get. The clothing fit surprisingly well, and part of me was surprised. How had the witches known? I made a mental note to ask them as I walked into the kitchen.

Vlad looked up and smiled. "Good morning. Care for some coffee?"

I took the mug and was surprised to find it was already full of coffee, made just the way I liked it. My eyebrow arched, questioning the gesture.

"I heard you leaving the bathroom and knew you would come here first. We have a busy day tonight." He smiled in the way he always did when he made a joke.

I smiled and took a sip. "Thanks, I appreciate it. I got your note last night after I had a strange talk with Mara." I chuckled. "Though, to be fair, most of my conversations with her are weird."

It was Vlad's turn to arch an eyebrow. "And?"

"For now, I'll trust this coven to have my back. Don't worry, I don't plan on going on a witch hunt or anything like that any time soon." I shrugged.

"Seriously though, Vlad. I shifted to save them. Why would I then turn around and murder them." I shook my head. "Give me some credit."

"I did. That's why I went to bed." He leaned back in his chair. "I hope you can learn to trust them. Once they bring someone in to their coven, it's a life-long relationship."

"I think we need to head back to HQ." I took a sip of heaven and sighed. "It's been too long and they need to know what's going on."

"I agree." Vlad picked up an empty plate and loaded it up with scrambled eggs, bacon, and toast before handing it to me. "You head to base and I'll check some leads."

"Thanks and are you sure?" I asked, raising an eyebrow as I took the plate. "You don't want to come with."

"Not really." He scowled. "There's a really good chance we'll have to do paperwork if we go. I'm hoping you have to do it."

"Oh, this was a bribe, was it?" I shook my plate at him.

"I suppose that's one way to look at it." He smirked. "My contacts don't take kindly to Feds."

"Um … pot calling kettle black?" I sat down

next to him and looked for a fork. Spying one, I snatched it up.

"I used to run with them, back before my time at the FBI," he explained as I took a bite of scrambled eggs. "They weren't too happy about my choice so I haven't seen them in a while. I think if I go without you they'll be fine though." He smiled. "I am me, after all."

I swallowed. "What about Mara? I thought you wanted to stay by her side until this was over?"

"I'll take her with me. She knew them as well back then. They'll be fine with her." He didn't look at me. In fact, he looked everywhere but at me. Was he embarrassed? Why?

"Why would they know anything about what's going on?" I asked. I hated when he kept things from me, especially since we were partners.

"Back when I knew them, we hung out with some shady characters. They tended to raise hell with a few really nasty werewolves. I'm betting they have heard some rumors about these wolves, at the very least." He looked like he might elaborate, but then just stopped and stared at me as I ate.

"If you see them commit a crime tonight, are you going to haul them in?" I asked, spearing a piece of sausage. I held it up between us. Then I took a bite.

"Nah, I don't care about their petty crimes and I'm sure the FBI won't care right now either." He watched me chew for a moment. "We have more important things to worry about than what they're into."

"Really? What types of crimes are they into? What was a typical Friday night like with Vlad and the gang?" I laughed, as I imagined him providing protection for rap stars at dance clubs.

The paranormal tended to drift more towards mafia types of crimes. They had a lot more power than most humans so it was easy to be the big bully, unless of course they changed their minds and decided to uphold the law, like Vlad had done a few years back.

He smiled. "A story for another time. Head off to command and get them to send us an entire SWAT team or a platoon of soldiers, if you can swing it. We're going to need them. Oh, and see if they have any radios we can use for communications."

"Are you really going to take Mara with you?" I asked as he got to his feet. "Will she be safe with them?"

"She's known them for a long time. They have respect for her and wouldn't dare mess with a great witch. She'll probably be safer with them than with us here." All the same, Vlad seemed to be worried about something. His forehead was creased with worry lines, and he scratched his chin.

"Hey, is something bothering you?"

"Nah." He shook his head. "It's nothing. Be safe."

Part of me wanted to press but I knew better. When Vlad clammed up, nothing could pry his mouth open. "Yeah, you too."

20

ALYSON

A fter I put my plate in the sink, I headed out to the garage to see if they had any cars I could borrow that weren't riddled with bullet holes. I found Brenda already in the garage and figured she was as good as anyone to ask.

"Hey, Brenda. Do you have an extra car I can borrow for the night? I need to head up to my base and report in."

"Sure, just try not to get into another firefight." Brenda chuckled and threw me a set of keys with a Hyundai logo on them. "It's hell to fix them, even with magic."

I clicked the key fob and saw a light for a small, sporty car out of the corner of my eye. "A Veloster? It looks like a tin can." I walked around the car and wondered how I was going to fit in it. I'm not too large but this thing sure seemed tiny, especially compared to my SUV.

Brenda laughed as she walked over. "Don't worry. You'll fit. It's rather comfy. The seat forms around a body quite nicely, and the car has some get up and go. Just try not to get shot while driving it."

"Can't I take out a SUV or a full-size sedan?" I hated tiny cars. They felt and looked like those toy cars my friends played with when I was a little girl.

"Sorry, since it's just you, it's the small car. We need to keep the larger vehicles here in case we need to make a quick exit." She gave me a conciliatory smile. "You know, all those extra seats."

She was right. If they were discovered, it would take every seat they had to get everyone to safety.

"Fine, I'll do my best to keep it safe. No promises on the gun fight." I grinned at her before having to practically sit on the ground when I got inside the thing.

She was right, it did have some get up and go.

Not many cars were on the road that night. I couldn't blame them. With all the chaos in the city, it felt like the apocalypse was already here. I wondered how it would feel if they finished the spell and all those demons showed up. This week would probably look like a walk in the park in comparison.

With the light traffic, it didn't take me too long to get to our local base of operations. Most FBI agents worked out of city offices but my division had a base set outside of town because we were special operations. Most of the cases we took were major crimes with a paranormal connection.

Sometimes we would fly out to investigate crimes in other regions of the country. We tried to keep the truth a secret from the world so if it was a paranormal crime, we were called in. It wouldn't do well to let people know everything they were afraid of was real. We made sure the paranormal secret stayed hidden while ensuring those same paranormals didn't cross the line. When they did, one way or another, we ended whatever the bad guys were doing.

"Strange, where are the guards?" I mumbled as I drove up to the unmanned security gate and swiped my badge over the pad, causing it to open.

Our compound was small. We usually had anywhere from fifty to two hundred and fifty agents on base, and even at night, there were always at least two guards on duty at the entrance, usually more.

No something was definitely wrong. Scanning the area around me as I drove up to the main building, I tried to assess the situation while telling myself it was just because everyone was out dealing with problems caused by the phones being down.

Still, there should have been people around. Most of the cars were gone, making the place look deserted as I pulled in. There were even tumble weeds billowing across the broken asphalt, though that happened more often than I cared to admit.

It was possible that most of the on-duty agents decided to head into the city to see if they could figure out what was going on, but there still should have been guards on duty. The place was never left unguarded, not even on holidays. There was way too much sensitive evidence and dangerous materials on hand, and besides, crime didn't take holidays.

I took a parking spot right outside of the main entry door, which wasn't even locked.

What happened here? Did the Shadow Walkers attack?

Even though it looked deserted, I knew I had to let Vlad know what was going on before I entered the building. Should something go wrong here, he wouldn't think I was missing until it was too late.

The problem was how could I let him know something was wrong?

I couldn't text or call him. Then a lightbulb went off in my brain. Our tracking beacons. One of mine was in my belt. I activated it and prayed he would receive the signal from the satellite in orbit.

Heaving a sigh, I straightened my shoulders and walked into the building with my senses on red alert. I almost wished there was enough room inside the building for me to transform into my dragon form. In my human form, my senses were excellent but as a dragon I could sense things impossible to normally detect. Plus, almost nothing could beat my fire and bulletproof scales.

The reception area was like most buildings, wide open with chairs in various locations throughout the room. On the walls were pictures of various monuments around our country. Three LCD TV screens were set up around the room. Normally, they played CNN, Fox News, and the third one alternated between the local news stations in LA.

When staffed, there were three uniformed security guards sitting behind the reception desk with multiple security screens showing them various locations on the grounds.

There was no sign of forced entry or fighting. The chairs and desks in the lobby were all in order. Other than the fact that no one was around and the front door was unlocked, it didn't look like anything was wrong. It just looked like everyone had gone home for the night.

Then I noticed the televisions were off, and only the emergency lighting was on. I wondered if the power had been cut. Maybe that was why no one was here.

Taking a deep breath, I picked up the tang of blood in the air. It was the first real indicator something wasn't right. Slowly, I pivoted around looking for any signs of struggle, including the blood I smelled. Nothing was out in the open.

The blood was coming from the reception area. Keeping an eye on the hallway to the left, I drew my Glock and walked to the right of the reception desk to see if the security cameras were working.

One of the regular security guards, Jimmy, was lying on the ground with a bullet hole to his head. His vacant expression told me he was long gone. I reached down anyway looking for a pulse. He was cold to the touch. The sight of him lying there like that pissed me off.

Jimmy had been a nice guy, a single father with

twin teenage boys. What would happen to them now?

As I stared at his corpse, I tried to keep a lid on my anger. It wouldn't help me to uncontrollably shift in a tight building. No, what would help would be finding the guys who did this.

Saying a quick prayer for the rest of my colleagues' safety, I headed down the right hallway toward the base commander's office.

The hallway was dark, and the overhead lighting was off here too. One of the security lights in the ceiling was blinking on and off, yet another indicator something bad had happened here.

My senses picked up movement ahead and the faintest of sound of footsteps. The hallway ahead ended in a T intersection. Behind the wall in front of me was a common room, usually where we held team meetings or ate lunches, but I didn't think the sound was coming from there.

Right or left? Before I made it to the end of the hall, I had to choose. If I went right, I would eventually get to my boss' office. Taking a left would send me to the gym, locker rooms, and IT. I chose right.

Listening for any noise before turning a blind corner, I put my back to the left wall before sticking my head and gun out into the hall to see if anyone was there. Nothing visible, but the stench of death wafted toward my nose. I had chosen the correct path.

My ears caught a squeak, like a rubber boot scraped on polished linoleum. Someone was here with me. I just didn't know where.

The path I was on ended and my only option was to turn left. While I wasn't sure if someone was around the corner, I wasn't quite sure how to check. Without lights, I couldn't use the mirror up in the top corner of the ceiling to see around the other side. Not even the emergency lights were on in this corridor.

Thankfully, I had excellent vision, even in the dark. I readied my weapon and squatted down before leaning around the corner. Good thing, too. A spray of bullets went right above my hair, tearing an erratic upward path into the wall above me. Without hesitating, I fired my gun into the chest of the man who had just tried to kill me.

He fell back and hit the ground as the M16 in his hands tumbled onto the linoleum. I quickly scanned in front and behind me for anyone else. Not seeing anyone, I made a grab for the weapon.

Whoever else was here would come running.

The report from an M16 is pretty loud inside a building, and my Glock wasn't exactly quiet. I doubt anyone would have missed our exchange. Once I had the pilfered rifle slung around my shoulder, I moved forward with my ears open and eyes scanning every shadow around me.

My path led me to a side door to the common room. It was closed. I put my head up against the door, straining to listen for any more intruders. My sensitive ears picked up a muffled sound, but I couldn't quite make it out. I wasn't sure if it was someone gagged trying to let me know they were in there or if someone was trying to whisper so low they sounded like a muffled voice.

I needed to take a prisoner, only one. Answers were needed and one of these intruders should be able to inform me what happened here. Since I knew someone was on the other side of the door, I had to enter.

Putting my hand on the handle, I turned it as slowly as possible, trying to keep from making any noise. The handle turned just fine. When I pushed the door open a little, it squeaked, letting whoever was in the room know exactly where I was and what I was doing.

"Mike? That you? Who'd you kill?" I heard a

man whisper as I continued to slowly open the door.

That whisper let me know exactly where he stood so I swung open the door swiftly and shot him in the thigh with my Glock. As long as I missed his artery, he would live, but the shot would still take him down, making him a great candidate to interrogate.

My victim screamed as he fell to the ground.

I couldn't make out any more forms in the room other than furniture but that didn't mean there wasn't anyone else hiding in here. Then again, no one was shooting at me either. I waited a few more seconds before pushing into the room.

The guy I shot just kept screaming and wailing, which while understandable was definitely going to draw attention.

"Shh, if you keep quiet I'll help you," I whispered to the guy as I kneeled next to his injured leg.

"Why would you help me? You just shot me!" The guy on the floor whimpered.

"Because you have the answers I want. If you give me what I want, I'll wrap your leg so you don't bleed out. If you don't give me answers, I'll shoot you again." I needed the guy to be too afraid to say no. I could tell from his scent he was human, so I figured he was just a hired hand and wouldn't want to get shot again if he could help it.

"How do I know you won't just kill me after I give you what you want?" At least he was considering my proposition.

"You don't, but if you don't cooperate, you will definitely die here." I would make good on my threats. He was part of a team who infiltrated a secret FBI location and killed some of our people. I couldn't be sure how many, but at that point, it didn't matter. Besides, the cameras were off. "Hurry up."

"Fine," he relented, his voice ragged with pain. "What do you want to know?"

"Who are you working for?"

"Some shadow agency. I don't know their name. Just heard it was shadow-something." He must have been too far down the ladder to know much.

"How long ago did you guys infiltrate this FBI base?"

"Yesterday." His answer correlated with the condition of Johnny's body in the front.

"How many of you are here?"

"I don't know how many are left, but we started out with one hundred soldiers. They told us this place was empty with only a few security guards watching the place. They didn't mention your guards were highly trained agents. We lost some of our men but I don't know how many."

"What kind of idiots don't collect their own intel? Who are you guys?" They couldn't be a regular unit of mercenaries if they just took the word of whoever hired them.

"We're…"

A shot rang out from behind me, echoing past my shoulder and silencing the goon on the floor forever.

As I started to turn around and return fire, a tranquilizer dart hit me in the neck. My world spun, as I whirled, trying to attack my assailant. Only, I couldn't feel my arms anymore. The ground beneath me went sideways, and I crashed to the ground as darkness overtook me.

21

ALYSON

"Ooowwww." Everything was still black and foggy. My head hurt like it had been put in a vise and twisted until just before my skull popped.

What happened? Where was I?

I tried to move my arms and legs but they would barely move, worse, as I tried, something bit into my wrists and ankles.

"Tell us where she is," a disembodied voice demanded, and while that should have scared me, I was too confused to really process what was going on.

"Huh?" It hurt to open my eyes, let alone speak.

"The great witch. I know you were with her. Tell us where she is and we won't kill you." The voice was starting to become clearer and get closer.

"Go to hell!" My headache spiked as I spoke, but I didn't care. I wasn't telling him a damned thing.

An open hand smacked my face so hard, my neck cracked when it whipped around. The tang of my blood filled my mouth as I realized that he had split my lip.

My captor must have used something in his hand to make my lip bust. My skin was thicker than the normal human's and it took a lot more force to bust my skin than a normal human's slap.

Before I could full process the situation, a fist punched the same side of my face. I felt metal graze along my cheek bone. He had to be using brass knuckles or something like it. It didn't help that this guy was strong too, but I wasn't going to give in.

"Up yours, you filthy piece of trash!" I knew my head was going to pay the price, but it wasn't nearly as painful as the last time I spoke. Hopefully, it meant whatever they had injected into my neck was burning out of my system.

This time he hit me from the other side of my face. He must not have known who or what I was. No shifter would give from just a few smacks, even if the interrogator used brass knuckles. We were all much tougher than this.

"I won't ask you again—"

The man was cut off before he could finish his statement by gunfire punctuated by a blood-curdling scream.

"Go, take care of him," my tormentor yelled right before his head twisted with a sickening crunch. As his corpse hit the ground, a blurry outline appeared in front of me.

"Alyson, are you all right?" It sounded like someone was yelling at me from a tunnel.

"What?" I shook my head and squeezed my eyes. It looked like Vlad was in front of me but he was too blurred to confirm visually. "Vlad?"

His natural spice and cinnamon scent flooded into my head and made me feel safe. He really was here to save me. No matter what my eyes said, the wonderful aroma in front of my face could only be from one person, Vlad.

I felt his hands around my arms and ankles, massaging them as the pressure from the restraints disappeared. "Yes, I'm here. You're safe now. Can you stand up?" He put his hands under my arms and tried to get me to stand up.

Instead I fell back on the chair. "I'm tied up."

"No, you aren't," he whispered soothingly. "You should be able to stand. What did they do to you?"

"Tranq dart." I exhaled slowly. "Otherwise I'd be dead."

"Crap, they must have given you an elephant tranquilizer. Here, drink this. It will help." Vlad put his wrist up to my mouth.

I tasted the metallic tang of blood and spit it out. "I'm not a vampire, blood doesn't help me."

"It's my blood, Alyson." Vlad's voice was a few octaves lower or maybe my hearing was going. "Come on, drink a bit more." He put his wrist back to my mouth and ran his hands down my back. The motion was comforting. I trusted Vlad to only give me what I needed and no more.

After taking a few sips, I couldn't stand it anymore though when I pulled away, I did feel better. "Wow. I had no idea your blood would make me feel so good. I'm not going to be turned, am I?"

"No, I can only turn humans. A shifter only gets the medicinal effect. It should give you strength to get up and get out of here." As Vlad helped me up, I felt stronger, better than normal. My vision was cleared, and I could see that they had moved me to the base's gymnasium. Idiots. They should have killed me.

"Hmm." I stretched and realized I must have

been out of it for a while. "How long ago did you get my message?"

As I asked that, I looked around. Vlad had been busy. There were over a dozen dead bodies littering the floor.

"How did you do this? Did you have back-up?" I knew he was strong and fast, but this was crazy.

"Alyson, I would never let my partner be hurt. When I received your signal a few hours ago, I came as quickly as I could." His fingers lightly moved the hair out of my face.

Something in my stomach fluttered at his touch. When he took his hand away, I actually missed it.

"Let's focus on getting out of here." He led me out of the gym with his hand on the small of my back.

"Vlad, did you come across anyone else alive? Any of our colleagues?"

"No, I found a few more dead bodies. You were the only friendly still alive. I'm sorry." He took my hand and squeezed it.

I squeezed his hand back. My heart was breaking for all the lost lives. I always felt more comfortable around humans than he did. In fact, I felt more comfortable with humans than I did any other paranormal creature, aside from Vlad.

There wasn't time to mourn the loss of my co-workers though. I had to put aside these feelings until after we solved this case. Because, right now, anger was the only emotion I could afford.

"Here, take these." My partner handed me my service pistol and an M16.

"Where did you get these?"

"From your captors. Come on." He led me toward the exit.

I wasn't sure if he'd gotten everyone or not, so I kept my eyes and ears open for anyone else.

What I couldn't stop dwelling on was how amazing I felt. That small amount of his blood made me feel ten years younger and in much better shape than I was. It still grossed me out but, dang, I felt great!

The smallest movement brought me out of my thoughts, a finger twitching on a trigger.

"Move!" I shouted as I shoved Vlad to the side. Even as our attacker fired at us, I was taking a shot at him with my Glock. Thankfully, Vlad's blood gave me an edge. While our attacker's shot buried itself in the spot behind where I'd been only a moment ago, my bullet slammed into his chest. Perfect shot.

He was dead before he hit the ground.

"Man, I need one alive to question," I growled, suddenly annoyed with my accuracy. "Do you think there are more? We need more answers." I wished I had more time with the guy I shot in the leg before his own people killed him.

"I managed to get us some answers. Not all of them but enough for the moment. Let's get out of here. I have a lead, and we need to go pick up Mara. I left her with my friends when I received your distress call." Vlad took point and headed toward the exit again.

"You what? Are you sure those guys will take care of her?" I couldn't believe he left Mara with criminals. Although, she could probably take care of herself, depending on how many of them there were. "By the way… they are after Mara. Before you arrived, they were asking me for her location." I really wished Vlad would have left one alive for us to question, but I was very grateful he came when he did.

"Did you tell them?" Vlad quirked an eyebrow at me as we made our way out of the building.

"What do you think? Those were humans. All they did was hit me a few times. I doubt there's even any evidence left on my face." I put my hand up to my lips and felt a fat lip, but the rest of my face felt fine.

Vlad turned and looked at me with worry in his eyes. "You might have some bruising but my blood should fix it before we meet up with Mara. Are you all right? They didn't do anything else, did they?"

"Vlad, thank you. I'm fine. I woke up right before you got to us. They had just started questioning me. I told them to go to hell and that was about it." I shrugged and turned around to make sure we didn't have anyone behind us.

For the moment, it was all clear.

22

ALYSON

As we exited the room, Vlad's left fist went up, indicating I needed to stop. I couldn't hear anything so he must have seen something when I was looking behind us.

"What?" I whispered so low only Vlad could hear.

"Movement up ahead and to the right." My partner took a step forward and I followed, scanning the area to the right.

I stopped and took in a deep breath. A familiar scent filled the air around us.

"Werewolves." Vlad's face changed back into his fighting form.

He was right. It smelled of death and sewer, just like when we went up against them before. These were no ordinary werewolves, they were the

Shadow Walkers. Here, at our base. I had to stomp down on my dragon's desire to come out and attack.

"My captors must have contacted their leader while I was knocked out. Why else would they be here?" I wondered if they knew I was a dragon shifter. I really hoped that wasn't true, that they just needed Mara so badly they came to interrogate me in person.

"I don't know but we need to follow their scent and see what they're up to." My partner ran ahead before I could respond, and I had to hurry to catch up to him.

Instead of heading to the exit which was only two right turns away, we headed left and back toward the offices where I was originally trying to go when I was captured.

While I was less worried about getting tranquilized with Vlad here, I still didn't like this. These magic-wielding werewolves were tough to fight. I had to shift to my dragon form for us to beat them last time, and that was with a contingent of trained witches. Worse, even if I wanted to shift, there wasn't enough room inside the building to allow it.

Gripping my M16, I took a step forward, and as I did, the smell and taste of magic, like warm earth on a spring day, hit me. I swallowed. Hard. Mara's magic.

I pulled on Vlad's shirt to stop him from barging ahead, and as he turned around and looked at me with furrowed brow, I put my finger up to my lips.

"Shh." I pointed to my nose and mouth and mouthed "Mara" and I could see the anger spread over Vlad's face. His eyes turned their freaky red and his fangs elongated.

A growl that made my fight or flight senses kick in rippled from his lips, and I had to wrangle my dragon under control. Vlad hadn't set off a need to shift since we first met.

Vlad had an inner demon he never wanted me to see, but I had seen it once. It was something I kept from him, but on a previous case involving children, he let lose in order to save a little girl. I was grateful she had passed out before Vlad showed up.

In his demon form, he grew in size, almost like a shifter, and he was exceptionally vicious. It dawned on me that this was how he saved me. He took that form and killed the men holding me. That was why he was so vague on how he killed so many humans.

"Vlad, I'm right behind you," I whispered,

hoping none of the other paranormals could hear me. That was all Vlad needed to know. It was go time.

Without responding, Vlad kicked the door inward, ripping it off its frame and sending it flying into the room. He followed it, leaping on the closest werewolf and tearing into him with all the strength his vampiric muscles could bring to bear.

As his claws tore outward in a vicious arc that ripped open the werewolf's stomach and spilled his entrails across the linoleum, the few werewolves who hadn't been in their wolf man form, shifted and charged him.

I took the opening to try to get to Mara. Darting into the room, I raised my M16, putting a three second burst into the brainpan of the were-wolf holding her prisoner. As his life evaporated into a red mist and his body collapsed to the floor, I sighted on his buddy. The other werewolf was already moving, already charging, and as he leapt for me, I emptied the weapon into his chest. Blood sprayed out his back right before his body crashed into me, knocking me to the ground beneath his bulk.

He wasn't dead, but he was hurt bad. Unfortu-nately, he didn't seem to care. As blood gushed from his torn open chest, he snapped at me. I dodged and drove my forehead into his snout. The sound of cracking bone filled the air, and as the werewolf slumped toward me dazed, I shoved him off.

I scrambled to my feet as Vlad flung one of the other werewolves through the air. It hit the wall between me and Mara with enough force to crack the drywall, and as it slid to the ground, shaking its head, it saw me.

A howl erupted from its throat as it leapt at me. This time, I sidestepped and used my now empty M16 as an improvised club. The butt of the weapon smashed into the underside of the creatures chin with enough force to knock him on his back, and as he crashed to the ground, I drew my Glock and put two into his skull.

As I stepped over the dead wolf, two burly men, the last of the wolves who hadn't shifted, grabbed hold of Mara. I smelled her magic in the air, but it didn't seem to matter. Golden bands began to glow on her wrists and ankles, and even though they flared like star fire, they somehow suppressed whatever spell she was trying to do.

Without her magic, there was nothing she could do, and the two quickly pulled her through the emergency exit.

I ran forward, trying to get to her. "Mara!"

A werewolf slammed into me, tackling me to the ground. Using our momentum, I managed to roll on top of the thing as we tumbled across the floor. The beast swiped at my legs with his claws. They ripped clean through my pants and sliced through my flesh.

Biting back the pain, I pointed the Glock at him and pulled the trigger. He slumped to the ground as blood blasted out of the freshly-minted hole in his head.

I rolled off the giant bag of bones to find that one of the men had remained behind. Worse, he'd shifted now. He lunged to bite my head off but I kept low, under his attack as I pulled the trigger. My bullet hit its mark right into the soft spot of the jaw.

I was already past him as his body collapsed to the ground. I ran to the emergency exit where they had taken Mara. Busting out into the parking lot, I watched in horror as an unmarked helicopter was already taking off with Mara and her captor inside. I couldn't shoot it down, even if it was close enough, not without endangering Mara in the process.

I sprinted for the helicopter, and was about to shift and try and take it that way, when the loud report of two gunshots brought me back to the present, reminding me that Vlad was still fighting off six Shadow Walkers. I threw one last glance at the helicopter as it disappeared into the horizon before turning around to help my partner. We might still be able to save Mara, but if I didn't help Vlad now, he might not live past the next few minutes.

I burst back through the emergency exit to find Vlad facing off with the only two remaining Shadow Walkers. His fist lashed out, moving so quickly I could barely even follow the movement. His fist slammed into the right werewolf's stomach before bursting through the creature's back in a spray of crimson gobbets.

The werewolf's mouth opened and closed like a dying fish, right before Vlad jerked his arm sideways, using his claws to practically tear the creature in two.

As its body hit the ground, he spun, lashing out with his heel at its partner as the werewolf leapt at him. The upward arc of heel of his foot didn't catch the creature on the underside of its snout so much as it shattered its entire skull into a gooey mist.

Flames and Cauldrons! What kind of power did

my partner have in his demon form and why didn't he bring it out more often?

As the Shadow Walker's corpse fell to the ground, Vlad turned his demonic eyes on me. "Mara?"

"They took her," and as I spoke the words, the look he gave me made me feel guilty even though it wasn't really my fault.

23

VLAD

I hadn't wanted Alyson to see me like this, but I needed the strength this form afforded me. After all, after she'd risked her life by shifting to her dragon in front of everyone, the least I could do was to shift into my demonic form. If I didn't, I wouldn't deserve to call her partner or friend.

A soft hand touched my shoulder. "Vlad, you're awesome in this form. Why have you hidden it from me all this time?"

In a guttural and deep voice, I responded, "Because I'm a monster like this. I never wanted you to see me lose control."

"Hey, turn around," Alyson demanded.

"Alyson, we don't have time for this. We have to get Mara." I complied while keeping my head down, trying to hide my face as much as possible.

When my demon came out, my face had sharper features and small one-inch horns protruded on my forehead. Veins popped out alongside them and my fangs grew longer and thicker.

"Mara's gone, Vlad, a few more seconds won't hurt." She nodded to me as she stepped up to me. "You're a super warrior like this. Please don't hide from me." Alyson cupped my face in her hand and ran her thumb along one of my fangs. "And as far as I can tell, you haven't lost control." She smiled at me.

"Please, not like this. Don't touch my demon face." It hurt my heart to know she saw this face, the real me, but to have her touch me like this was too much.

"Vlad, you're handsome, inside and out. I wouldn't be a very good friend if I couldn't handle the way you look right now. Trust me, this doesn't bother me at all." She ran the tips of her fingers up along my horns and my blood pulsed with the sudden desire to take her. Alyson couldn't have known that the horns are an erogenous zone for most demons and vampires. "And you'll need this kind of power if we're going to save Mara."

MY EYES ROLLED to the back of my head and a growl came up from my chest of its own accord.

"Sorry, I didn't mean to hurt you." She pulled her hand back from my face and part of me wished she hadn't. Still, this was no time for foreplay. I had to focus on the case and ensuring the safety of our planet.

"What happened to Mara?" I asked, trying to get myself back under control.

"I'm sorry." She sucked in a breath and met my eyes. "They took her away in a helicopter. It was all my fault. I should have been faster." The look on my partner's face almost broke my heart.

"No, don't blame yourself. You did what you could. We have to trust that Mara knows what she's doing. There's no way they found her where I left her. She must have followed me here and turned herself in to them. After all, her original plan was to be captured by them for us to follow. I just hope that it works."

My face shifted back to its normal, human form. Even though Alyson said she was fine with my demon face, I wasn't fine with it. Guess, I was just broken that way.

"If they sacrifice her, we're done for." Alyson gestured at the mess of werewolf bodies littering the floor. "I don't know how many they have killed in their ritual so far, but they must be close by now. What do we do?"

"We find Mara." I gave my partner a sly smile. "The thing with Mara is you can never quite trust her to listen so I planted a tracker on her."

"You're a genius, if a bit of a jerk." She gave me a determined smile as she scooped up a new M16. "Come on, we can leave through the emergency exit."

Alyson ran to the door with me following close on her heels after I'd picked up my own rifle.

"I'll drive while you track her," Alyson suggested as she looked around for my car. "Um... which one is it." She paused. "No..."

"Yes." I nodded to the canary yellow 1970 Ford Mustang Boss 302 I had borrowed from my friends. "So much yes."

"Well, I'm still driving." She shook her head. "Should have gotten an SUV."

"Well, next time you pick out the car then." I smirked. "And I'm not sure you should drive. Every time you do, we end up crashing or blowing up." As Alyson gave me a faint scowl, my smirk turned into a smile. "Have at it."

I threw her the keys before sitting in the

passenger seat. After buckling up, I pulled out my phone and opened the satellite app. A few taps as Alyson revved the engine and I had the signal for the tracker not currently on my body.

Alyson and I both wore multiple trackers with the idea that a search might find one or two but not all of them. When I was searching for her while she was captured, I noticed one of her beacons was in a different part of our base. They must have found it and moved it, hoping to put any rescuers off the trail. It didn't help them. All I had to do was find the blip with the most transponders in one place and voila! It was easy.

"Got a lock on Mara," I announced. "She's stopped now. They must have just landed somewhere not far from us. Over in the valley? Who uses the valley for a secret base?" The valley was full of homes and small businesses. A helicopter landing would stand out there.

"Well, that's just great," Alyson said as she got onto the 134 freeway and headed to Sherman Oaks. "Fighting a contingent of Shadow Walkers right in the middle of suburbia is definitely less than ideal."

24

ALYSON

We drove to our destination in silence. I hoped Vlad wasn't worried about me seeing his demon face. It was so powerful. Yes, a bit scary, but exciting too. To be honest, it was kind of a turn on.

"Am I still on the right track?" I had been driving for almost thirty minutes without any changes to direction. Sherman Oaks wasn't exactly a supervillain hotspot. It seemed like a really odd place to have a lair. There were a lot of paranormal creatures who lived there in harmony with each other and the humans, but none of the ones I knew about had ever tried to jumpstart the apocalypse.

"Yes, we're almost there," Vlad responded. "I find it difficult to imagine their lair here in the middle of the valley. It must be another ritual site."

I hadn't considered their need for another ritual. Mara couldn't be the one they intended to sacrifice here. As far as I knew, she had no close ties to anything in the valley, but she could be forced to watch as they sacrificed other beings or possibly even witches. If she was having another senior moment, they might even be able to persuade her to give over some lost information regarding the spell. She did have knowledge of it, after all.

"Take a right up here, and we should drive right past where her beacon is located." Vlad put his phone away and began scanning the area.

I slowed down after I made the turn and tried to see if I could find anything looking like a ritual killing site. "There!"

I pointed to the left at an old abandoned restaurant. It matched up with Vlad's description and would have been a perfect place for a deadly ritual.

"Drive around the block and see if anything else pops out. Her beacon is coming from here, but I want to make sure we aren't heading into a trap. If they found my beacon on her, it's possible Mara isn't even here." As he spoke, Vlad shifted into his vampire form, but kept from going full demon, presumably for the enhanced senses.

"You know, I'm glad you're using your vampire

side, but if you need to go full demon again, go ahead and do it. I don't want you to feel the need to hide who you are. I know, I have to do it, and it sucks." I looked over at him. "You don't have to do it. Not with me anyway."

Vlad growled but didn't say anything as he began to scan the area with his bright red eyes. I guess that was my answer.

"Fine, just know I'm cool with him. Better you bring out your demon than I shift into a dragon." I turned left to head back around the block, checking for anything out of the ordinary, like that helicopter they'd used to escape.

"I'll do whatever is necessary to keep you safe but that doesn't mean I like my demon form. I much prefer to fight with this face." He touched his cheek. "It's a good compromise."

"Understood." I couldn't really blame him. If he didn't want to show that part of himself to others, it was his choice. "Wait, do you feel that?"

All of a sudden my chest felt like a ton of bricks had landed on it, and my breathing became difficult. Worse, the air started to taste of ozone and sulfur.

"The smell," I mumbled, gesturing toward the building. "It's as though a thousand corpses were rotting right here. The acrid scent actually hurts my nose."

"Yes." Vlad scrunched his nose. He had never done so before, at least not in front of me. It added a level of humanity to his vampire face, in an odd sort of way. His red eyes crinkled and when his nose scrunched, his mouth opened further to reveal even more of his fangs. Even with his vampire eyes and fangs, his face showed a human emotion I didn't normally see coming from Vlad - disgust. Something about it made him seem more human than he had since I'd met him.

I waved my hand in front of my face, trying to fan the stench of rotting meat away from me as we moved even closer to whatever was causing the smell and creepy feeling. If this wasn't the right place, well, I almost wasn't sure I wanted to know what that would feel like because this felt like Grade A evil.

"Could it be they're in the middle of another ritual?" It was all I could come up with. Never had I experienced something like this before. "Is your head pounding? Mine is." My eyes were starting to water as fear traveled up my arms and spine. I was smothered by fear, death, and evil. It was a devastating feeling. All I wanted to do was take a hot shower and clean off the filth I could feel coming from the restaurant.

Without warning, Vlad's demon form emerged. "Yes, in addition to a general feeling of disgust and a need to kill." He inhaled sharply through his nose. "Be careful, I can smell many Shadow Walkers."

I caught it out of the corner of my eye. He must have instinctually shifted to combat the surrounding evil. In a way, it helped to calm my nerves. Knowing he brought his deadliest form to the battle was comforting.

Still, it was probably a good idea if I kept my mouth shut in regards to his current form. I wasn't sure if he knew he had shifted, and I needed him to focus on the fight, not his insecurities.

I pulled over to the side of the street where the power was the strongest. Might as well get as close as I could before leaving the safety of our car. When I stepped out, I couldn't help but rub my arms, trying to get an invisible layer of filth off of me.

Vlad checked his weapons, and I did the same.

"Should we try calling for backup again?" Vlad asked in his deep, demon voice. "I know I just tried a few minutes ago, but maybe it will work."

"I doubt we're going to get through." I shook

my head, wishing it wasn't true. "Something tells me no one will get through to anyone before this spell has been cast and after that, I doubt it will matter." It had to be a magical curse keeping the phones out of commission, otherwise they'd already be working.

"Ready? I don't know how much help Mara will be but we need to try and free her. Hopefully, she can provide some degree of magical cover and stop whatever they're doing inside." Vlad pulled a foot long Becker BK7 knife from a sheath on his waist in addition to unholstering his Glock. Part of me didn't understand since he had razor sharp claws, but then again, maybe he was going to throw it or something.

"Ready as I'll ever be. Let's burn this place down." I took point and led the way. In one hand, I held a fully loaded M-16 I picked up on our way out of our base. In my pockets were two full ammo magazines for the assault rifle as well as a sheathed KA-BAR USMC fighting knife I'd pulled off one of the enemy combatants for close combat.

The building in front of us had at one time been a Chinese restaurant. It looked like a little pagoda with crumbling red tiles on the roof. We entered from the back, past two large rolling dumpsters overflowing with rotten food and who knew what else. Flies were all over the place. My skin crawled with the thought of what might be in those trash bins.

I looked to Vlad who seemed to be on the verge of getting sick, just like me. His nostrils flared, and he grimaced while shooing flies away from his face. If only his natural scent was strong enough to cover what was coming from this place, I would have had my nose in his chest, or neck, just to get rid of the stench. Vlad probably would have welcomed my scent as well. He told me once I smelled like a winter wonderland, whatever that meant.

I felt his body heat along my back before he spoke softly in my ear. "You open the door, and I'll go in first."

I nodded twice, taking a deep breath to clear my head before pulling the door open.

Vlad burst in the second it was wide enough, and his entrance was followed almost immediately by the screech of an alarm going off. So much for surprise.

25

ALYSON

"Vlad, to the right. The magic feels the darkest coming from there." I pointed with the muzzle of my weapon while trying to ignore the effect the alarm was having on my heightened hearing.

He moved silently, even though we didn't need to be silent anymore. Everyone within a two block radius had to hear the alarm bells going off. The sound was so loud and grating, it gave me a headache.

Thankfully, it seemed to be having the same effect on the inhabitants. A few agonizing howls split the air as the wolves within attempted to get away from the high pitched frequency of the alarm. I was actually surprised the Shadow Wolves hadn't turned it off yet, but then again, maybe they were planning on killing us first.

The taste and smell of evil magic snaked through the corridor we were in. It felt like black vines weaving their way along my body and strangling every inch of me. We were barely inside the place and I was already having a tough time moving forward.

Something was constricting against my chest and when I brought my hand up to see what it was, I only felt my shirt. It had to be a spell or enchantment over this place, but it felt real nonetheless.

We came to the end of the corridor, and the only way to go was left. I followed the path and it opened into what I think used to be the kitchens, now filled to the brim with Shadow Walkers. The room had been gutted. Even though the ceiling was only ten feet tall, all of the interior walls save one had been removed to make this one giant room.

No one seemed to notice us as we approached, or if they did, they didn't care, which was good because there were almost two dozen Shadow Wolves within. Most of them were crowded inside a massive crimson circle painted on the floor, and the alarm only seemed to be bothering the few standing outside it. Was it some sort of sound blocking spell?

It certainly seemed like it, and as I watched them move, the rest of the Shadow Wolves crowded inside it.

As the Shadow Walkers crowded around a large pentagram painted on the floor, I gulped. There was no way we'd be able to take this many out, especially since this place was too small for me to shift.

Worse, the largest werewolf I had ever seen stood in the center. He must have been close to ten feet tall and even on all fours, his back had to be as high as I was tall. His fur was a deep charcoal gray, almost black, with a silver stripe down its back.

Turning my attention from them, I spied Mara sitting on a chair in a corner of the room with three furry guards. Her arms were crossed over her chest and her face was pinched, but otherwise she seemed fine. Another circle had been painted around them, making me think it was definitely some kind of sound deafening ritual. Probably to keep anyone from hearing Mara if she decided to scream for help.

There were six regular werewolves in another corner, all bound and gagged with three Shadow Walkers guarding them. That combined with the

fear in their eyes, made me think they were innocent prisoners.

Shifting my gaze back to the pentagram, I saw a
man move next to the huge Shadow Walker. He
held an old leather book which appeared to be
falling apart at the seams. With the alarms going
off, I couldn't hear what he was saying but I did see
his mouth moving.

The moment he stopped speaking, the alarms
stopped as well. There were a few seconds where
the entire room was devoid of any sounds at all,
almost as though I had gone deaf. A feeling of
vertigo rushed through me, and when I had to put
my hands out to stop myself from falling over, Vlad
put a hand on my shoulder helping to stabilize me.

All eyes in the room turned to Vlad and me in
unison. It was such an eerie feeling to have everyone
looking at me with blank expressions. I got the
impression they were all under a spell and doing as
someone bid them to do. No one moved on their
own, except the man in the middle of the pentagram.

His smarmy smile was unsettling to say the
least. "Ah, just the guest I was waiting for. Thank
you, Alyson, for joining us. We couldn't finish this
ritual without you."

"Well, it seems my invitation to the party was lost. Sorry, didn't mean to be late." I shrugged, trying to play it off even though I was suddenly very worried. While I could always shift and fight my way through this, doing so might kill my friends. "Since you know who I am, care to tell me who you are?"

"Please forgive my rudeness. My name is Quincy Silverton. I'm a Halfling, and this is my coven." He lifted his arms indicating the Shadow Walkers.

"Ah, so you're what? Pissed at your mom? Dad? Because they didn't bring you into their coven? Is that what this is all about?" I snorted. "Seems a little extreme to me."

From what Mara had told me about halflings, it would make sense for this guy to find some other outcasts to bond with but this was just over the top crazy. Who works so hard to destroy the world just because their parents sucked?

Quincy chuckled. "No, it's nothing so mundane as a family squabble. This is about power." He looked me up and down. "Now that I have you, I will be the most powerful being in all of the universes."

"Multiverse theory?" I myself had thought it possible at one time. "Not that again."

His beady little eyes scanned me from head to foot. "So smart. It's too bad the spell will kill you. You would have made for a wonderful associate." He sighed. "Ah well. Can't have an omelet without breaking a few eggs."

I almost gagged as my body shivered from disgust. "Sorry, gonna have to take a raincheck on that." I thumbed over my left shoulder to indicate where I had last felt Vlad. "My partner and I are here to stop you."

As Quincy's gaze flicked behind me, he laughed. "Your partner was smarter than you gave him credit for. It seems he has decided to abandon you to your fate. He couldn't have helped anyway. We are too strong now. We've already completed ninety-nine sacrifices. Once the final one is cast, there is no stopping the spell."

While his words rattled me, I trusted Vlad to have my back, no matter what. He must have found a way to get to Mara or to do something else to stop this madman.

Quincy must have known I was a dragon shifter. That was why they chose this confined place. It would be almost impossible for me to shift in here safely. Those two Shadow Wolves who escaped from Mara's lair obviously made it back to tell their boss about me, after all.

"I hate to burst your bubble but you won't be sacrificing me. My fate is to stop you and your furry little band of misfits." At least, I hoped that was my fate. 'Fake it 'til you make it' that was my motto that day. Besides, he was not going to have the pleasure of seeing my fear or any lack of confidence in beating him.

If Vlad could get Mara out, I would shift and burn this place to the ground. If I was meant to be the final sacrifice, I had to do whatever I could to keep them from killing me, even it meant hurting some innocents in the process. If I didn't, they would die no matter what. All the same, I would do everything I could to save everyone.

Unfortunately, it seemed like my choices were to save either the Earth or my friends. That was unacceptable, especially since I didn't know what Vlad was up to. For all I knew, he has a way out of this mess, and despite what Quincy had said, I knew Vlad hadn't abandoned me.

He was too honorable to do so. Plus, Mara was still here. No matter how my partner felt about me, Vlad would never leave his old girlfriend to die here. I had to trust that he was working out a plan to save Mara and me.

The Shadow Walkers around the circle began to growl while the guards stood still. It was the first time since I entered they hadn't acted as one unit. Was it intentional or did Vlad do something to distract the others?

"Like the other dragons, no one can save you." Quincy nodded at me and the three Shadow Walkers closest to me broke the circle and came after me. "It's time for your kind to be exterminated. Once and for all."

"Wait, do you mean to tell me you know what happened to the others?" I swallowed, leaving the rest of the question unsaid, my family?

"Of course." Quincy smiled at me right as three Shadow Walkers leapt at me. "I'm responsible for their deaths." His grin widened. "Well, mostly."

"You what?!" I cried. Rage exploded through me as I raised my M16 and shot the first two in the head, ending their lives in sprays of blood and bone.

The third landed a few feet from me, and as he stood up on his hind quarters, I blasted him in the chest. My rounds ripped through the monster's chest, turning it into a mishmash of bloody hamburger, but they didn't slow him down.

Aiming for his head, I got off one more shot before he swiped his oversized paw at my weapon, knocking my shot wide and causing the burst to tear into the Shadow Walkers on the outside of the circle. They didn't even flinch as the bullets tore into them.

Barely keeping a grip on the rifle, I drew my knife in my off hand and aimed for the underside of the massive maw on the Shadow Walker in front of me. He deflected the thrust to one side with a painful swipe across my forearm, causing my blade to scrape along his muzzle.

I ducked his next swipe and twisted to one side of the wolf, managing to plunge my knife into his rear hip. He howled, more in surprise than pain, as two more of his buddies came at me. Before they made it to me, I put a round into the head of the monster I had been fighting.

"Don't kill her, just subdue her," Quincy ordered as the werewolf collapsed to the ground. "We need her for the ritual!"

Spinning back to my new friends, I squeezed off another few rounds, hitting one of the attacking wolves in the eye. As it dropped lifelessly, the other one grabbed me by the throat. My M16 slipped from my hands, catching on the strap around my shoulder.

As he lifted me up, his clawed fingers squeezing around my neck, I pulled my Glock from its holster and shoved it under his snout with one swift motion. Before the Walker could realize his error, I pulled the trigger. Warm blood and thicker bits splattered across my face.

The Shadow Wolf dropped me, on account of having most of his head removed by force, and even though my legs were a little rubbery from lack of oxygen, I scrambled away. Holstering my Glock, I brought my M16 up, intent on firing at them if they came at me again.

"Enough!" Quincy bellowed. "The rest of you, grab her but don't kill her yet. It must be me who drains her blood inside the circle."

I had only made a dent in the number of evil wolves so I needed Vlad to jump in soon and help. If they all rushed me together, there was no way to fight them all off without shifting, and if it came to that, I'd do it, consequences be damned.

"Drain this," I snarled, unloading the M16 at Quincy. The bullets just bounced off his shield in a spray of lavender sparks. Flames and cauldrons, he was going to be difficult to kill if he had a shield strong enough to repel gunfire. Then again, bullets were one thing, and dragon fire was another.

As the wolves charged, I decided to spray and pray. I wasn't sure if I killed the ones I hit or not but I would take what injuries I could. With the limited ammunition I had, there was almost no chance I could kill them all with bullets alone.

I scanned the room and still didn't see Vlad anywhere. At least I finally caught sight of Mara, sitting in the corner opposite of the imprisoned werewolves, not moving. Had Quincy bound her somehow?

Retreat was my only option so I turned around and ran back the way I came hoping to see Vlad.

He was nowhere in sight so, for the moment, I was on my own. Once I was next to the exit door, I turned around and emptied my M16 at the wolves as they came. They were so large, only one at a time could come down the hallway. It was a bottleneck for them and a win for me.

Shooting at each head when it made its way around the corner, I managed to down a few more before they finally grew wise to my tactics. Even still, there had to be over a dozen left and that didn't even count Quincy.

While they weren't the smartest creatures, they did seem to learn from their mistakes. So far, they seemed to mainly rely on their strength and numbers. I hoped that brains would win out in the end if I could just last long enough to outsmart them.

In front of me was a pile of dead oversized wolf shifters. It would be difficult for me to get back inside through them and I had to assume the Walkers would be coming for me either through the pile or around through the front. My only choice was to go around the building and see if there was another door I could get into before I was caught.

Sure, I could have fled. I could have run outside, shifted, and flew off. Maybe that would have been the smart move to save the world from Hell, but I had a job to do and a duty to protect the innocent. I couldn't abandon those wolves and Mara to Quincy and his cult.

26

VLAD

I hated not being able to tell Alyson my plan. Normally, I would have texted what I was up to. With the phones out, there was no way I could tell her that wouldn't clue in the Walkers.

As we entered the back of the restaurant, I had noticed a ladder leading up to the roof. This building was old enough and in bad enough shape that I thought I might be able to make a hole or two through the roof and get Mara out of the way.

Something wasn't right with her. She would never sit so still, looking mad at the world like that. I could only assume Quincy had bound her in some way with his magic. If his magic was able to hold her so long, he had to be just as strong or stronger than the great witch.

Still, he was only a halfling. There was no way

he had enough magic on his own to best the greatest witch alive. The only possibility was if her growing senility had overwhelmed her rational mind. In such a moment of weakness, he could have struck.

I would find out, one way or the other.

So, as soon as I got a glimpse of the room layout and where the prisoners were, I ghosted back to the ladder. While I hated leaving Alyson alone without a word as to why, Alyson was stronger than she realized. I knew she would be able to protect herself against those wolves.

Once I was on the roof, I looked for a weak spot over the area where Mara and the other innocent victims were. There was evidence of water damage in the front corner and that would make it possible for me to make a hole large enough to get inside and get Mara out, but it would be loud. If only I could contact Alyson and have her make some sort of distraction.

I should have realized that all I had to do was wait. I heard gunfire erupt downstairs. Lots of gunfire. Alyson was using her M16, good. I worked fast, pulling off the tile and ripping away at the wood underneath me. It came off faster than I expected. Thankfully, the wood was rotted all the way through.

Looking down through the opening in the roof I was stumped. The image below me was very different from the image of Mara I saw when inside of the room just a few moments ago.

This view showed me Mara standing and moving her hands around as though she was weaving an intricate spell. Could it be she used a glamour to make it look like she was frozen in the corner? Glamours were pretty low-level stuff. I would have expected Quincy to pick up on it, even if it was the most powerful glamour in the world.

"Pst," I whispered, hoping to catch Mara's attention.

Mara looked up and smiled. She nodded and kept going with whatever she was doing. I knew from my previous time with Mara that I needed to stay where I was until she was done. The radius of the glamour was too confining to accommodate me. When I jumped down there, the glamour would break and everyone would know Mara was free.

I stuck my head through the hole in the ceiling and watched as Alyson shot the Shadow Walkers down one at a time. When they all turned and attacked Alyson as one, I almost abandoned Mara to help her.

The only thing that stopped me was when I saw how they all stopped and had to enter the corridor one at a time. Alyson could take them down that way relatively easily. It was like fishing in a tank.

Everyone's attention was on the back of the room and the fight with Alyson. It was the perfect chance to get Mara out of there.

"Mara, you ready?" I whispered down to her.

She looked up to me and winked before holding up a finger, indicating she needed a moment longer.

I wasn't sure how much more time we had. Alyson would either be overwhelmed in just a few minutes or Quincy would intervene before all of his soldiers were killed.

Mara looked up and said, "Now."

I jumped down and looked around. No one had noticed my presence. When I looked to Mara for explanation, she held a finger up to her lips. It really didn't matter, as long as I got her up on the roof before anyone noticed. From there, we could see about getting the rest of the innocents out.

Mara climbed on my back, and I jumped up and grabbed the outer edge of the wall where it met the ceiling. After I pulled us up, Mara climbed off my back.

"Be very careful. After what I did to it, this roof is about to collapse. We have to jump down over the edge in case it caves in before we make it to the back where the stairs are located." I knew Mara couldn't land safely on her own, so I motioned for her to get on my back again.

Instead, Mara went down to her knees and looked inside. "Wait, I need to see where Alyson is. We must get the regular werewolves in the other corner out. I've seen what happens. They are in danger." After a moment, she looked back up at me. "She must be around back still. We have only a few minutes. Help me to save them." Mara stood up and began walking across the dangerous roof to the other side.

"Wait, what do you mean you've seen what happens? Did you have a premonition?" I knew she had the ability, but thought she had lost it decades ago.

The great witch didn't break stride as she moved toward the corner of the roof over the wolves. "Yes, dear. Lately, I've seen quite a few things. Fate has decided to shine on me for this particular case. Now help me!"

"Stop, Mara. Come down with me, and I will go around to their side and get them to safety. The roof is going to collapse if you walk across it." I couldn't save her only to have her drop right back inside the lion's den.

She took a step and her foot got stuck in the red tiles. It almost went all the way through. With a sigh, I made my way to her and helped her get her foot out of the roof.

Mara let out a vaguely embarrassed sigh and relented. "Yes, you may be right, but we must hurry. Time is not on our side."

I nodded. "Here, put your hands on my shoulders and I'll carry you out."

I grabbed her around her waist and gently lifted her until her feet were clear of the dangerous red tiles. Once she was safe on my back, I went over the edge, landing heavily but safely in the lot below. The second our feet hit the ground, Mara slid off my back and moved to the front of the building.

I had to stop her before Quincy and his cult saw her through the front windows. "Mara, hold up. Let's be a bit more careful here. You don't want the enemy to see you through the front windows." I ran behind her and almost tripped when I looked inside. They wouldn't be looking out at us any time soon. "Shi—"

"Language!" Mara interrupted, shaking her head in dismay. "Now, hurry up!"

"What is Alyson doing?" I knew now why Mara had insisted we hurry. The werewolves might not make it.

27

ALYSON

It was a good thing I exited the building because it gave me the chance to see what Vlad was up to. I had circled around to the side where Mara was sitting and looked up when I heard a noise. It sounded like someone had slipped on some tiles and to my surprise, I saw Vlad up on the roof with Mara on his back.

With the both of them safe, I trusted Vlad to get the innocent werewolves out as well, letting me do what needed to be done. Since Quincy had already sacrificed ninety-nine paranormal creatures, I had to end this now. Even if he didn't get ahold of me, he would find someone else with enough magic to make the final sacrifice. Besides, the bastard had told me he was responsible for wiping out dragons. He had to answer for that too.

The only confusing part was this place. It meant nothing to me so why did he choose it to sacrifice me? Mara had said each location had to have significant importance to the being who was sacrificed. Maybe the last spot didn't matter? Either way, it was time I finished this.

Since there wasn't a door on this side of the building, I kept running around to the front of the building. It was unlocked, too. Mighty nice of Quincy to make it easy for me to get back inside.

When I opened the door, I realized why. Several Shadow Walkers were lined up next to the opening just waiting for me to arrive. Great.

Two of them grabbed my arms in the blink of an eye. I was hosed. I tried to pull my arms free but they were way stronger than I was in my human form. As I tried to pull away, they just clamped down even harder, causing my muscles to grind into my bones, and I realized that they might just be strong enough to break my arms.

If they succeeded, I wouldn't be able to fight back. I saw Mara through the front window and knew it was now or never. Once they got me further inside, I'd be done.

Removing my mental clamp on my dragon, I

shifted. I'd never tried shifting while someone was holding me before but luckily, it had the desired effect. The two men touching me were thrown violently back against the wall while I grew and grew.

My head smashed up against the ceiling, just like I thought. There wasn't any room to move around. My tail was hanging outside the door while my wings pushed several of the Shadow Walkers up against the walls.

Quincy was right in front of me. Behind him were the innocent werewolves. If I blew my fire now, they would burn too.

"Don't let her breathe fire! Get a fire extinguisher or something!" Quincy yelled as he threw a fireball at me.

Stupid man, fire doesn't hurt dragons. The magical blast splashed harmlessly against my scales. Still, Quincy obviously didn't understand my moral fiber, thinking I would incinerate him with innocents in the line of fire. Maybe I could use that to my advantage.

If Vlad was the partner I knew him to be, he was working on a way to get those werewolves out of this place before I brought it down. I just needed to give him some time.

"Give it up, Quincy." My voice was deep and guttural. "You've lost."

"I had hoped you wouldn't shift, but I was prepared." Quincy smirked before he threw his hands toward me.

A blue lightning bolt shot out from his hands and hit my chest. It wasn't painful, it felt more like a scratch. Only, as I tried to laugh at his puny power, I found myself unable to do so. My wings wouldn't move either. When I tried to swish my tail around, it wouldn't move. He'd froze me to the spot.

Flames and cauldrons!

If I couldn't move, he just might be able to drain me of my blood given enough time. Sure, I was outside of the circle, and it was unlikely he could move me, but maybe he didn't need me inside the circle for his spell.

In the corner, I watched as Vlad and Mara worked to get the werewolves out. The front window closest to the innocent wolves burst open, causing Quincy to turn and look in that direction. Before the halfling could throw another spell, Mara held up her hands in front of her. A shield of irides-cent energy sprang up before her while Vlad guided the wolves outside.

Normally, her shields were see-through but the

magic used to create this one was visible to me in my dragon form. A light pink glow surrounded the edges of a silver disc. It looked to be at least five feet wide and went from the floor to the ceiling.

Quincy threw his hands toward the shield and his blue lighting bounced off and hit the ground.

The werewolves were moving very slowly, and I wanted to scream at them to hurry but I couldn't say a word. My frustration was growing and smoke came out of my nostrils.

Quincy looked from one corner of the room to the other. "How'd you do it? I can still see you sitting in the corner? Astral projection?" Quincy continued to barrage Mara's shield and each bolt he sent bounced right off. One of the stray bolts hit one of his Shadow Wolves and he froze in place.

"A really great glamour. Guess you aren't so powerful after all, are you?" Mara laughed and walked backwards out of the broken window while keeping her shield up.

Hold up, smoke? Out of my nostrils?

I took in a huge breath of air and prepared to blow fire as hard as I could once Mara had made her way out of the building. If I could get enough air in, I could unleash the fire through my nose. I only needed to seriously injure Quincy to disrupt his concentration and end his spell. At least, that was the general consensus regarding spells.

Quincy was still in the middle of the circle. Would killing him there set off the end of the world or would it stop it?

Since I couldn't move, I needed to just roll the dice and pray I actually had good luck for once.

The second Mara disappeared from view, I forced air and flames up through my snout. If I had been in a human shape, I would have just scorched the ground but with the long muzzle of a dragon, two intense jets of flame blazed through the air, and the best part? He didn't even see it coming.

The jets of flame hit him square in the back, burning him to ash in the span of a second.

Just like that, I could move again. As Quincy's magic spell dissipated, I blew again, letting the full force of my flames hit the ground. Dragon fire covered the pentagram within his circle, burning away the blood and the ritual magic along with it.

The Shadow Walkers looked around dazed and confused, and when they saw me, they tried to flee. With a roar, I infused my rage into my breath and unleashed a blaze in their direction.

What remained of the evil wolf pack caught fire. As the entire building went up in flames, I swung my tail back and forth while I used my right wing to plow through the wall. Unable to take the impact, the entire building fell on me.

I burst my head out of the fiery rubble and took a deep breath. "Ahh, finally some fresh air." As my flames burned, the stench of evil began to disperse.

Flapping my wings as I pulled myself free, I flew up a few feet, just enough to get away from the burning building.

I could only hope the alarm earlier coupled with the evil magic that had permeated the area drove away anyone who might be close enough to see my dragon form.

Once I was clear of the fire, I shifted back into my human form. Agony I'd only experienced a few times in my life ripped through me, turning my blood to boiling magma, and causing my muscles to shriek and convulse as my inner dragon raged. Still, I had enough mental control to shove her back in her box, even if it felt like she was raking my brain with red hot pokers.

28

ALYSON

After I finished spitting up blood from my too quick transformation back into a human, I made my way back and began looking for my partner.

"Alyson, over here!" I looked to my right toward the voice, catching sight of Vlad two blocks down with Mara standing right behind him.

I ran over to them, and as I got close, Vlad pulled me into a bone crushing hug.

"Can't. Breathe," I wheezed out.

"Oh, sorry! I'm just so happy to see you made it out alive." Vlad pulled back but still held my shoulders.

"Thanks, I am too. For a few minutes there I wasn't sure I would make it. Great job with the whole glamour in the corner thing, Mara." I looked over to see Mara looking away from us. She was watching the building burn. I noticed her furrowed brow and something wasn't sitting right in my gut.

"Is everything all right?" I asked. "You look worried."

"Yes, yes. Great job." Mara turned around to look at us and asked, "Do you think Quincy was smart enough to pull this whole operation off? His Shadow Walkers definitely were not. They were strictly muscle."

"Totally strong muscle, but yes, I wondered that as well." I nodded. "Quincy seemed pretty smart, but your glamour really stumped him. Shouldn't he have been able to figure that one out?" Even I noticed something wasn't quite right when I first eyed Mara in the corner.

"He should have. However, if he was more focused on you, Alyson. He may not have even looked at me once I switched over to the illusion." The great witch looked back to the burning restaurant, clearly still concerned.

I followed her gaze. "Do you think the Walkers will survive this? I've never known anything to survive dragon fire, but with all of their dark magic, I wonder if they might."

I wouldn't want to see what they looked like if they did make it out. Third degree burns all over their body would not only be extremely painful but completely disfiguring as well. Then again, they were werewolves. Maybe they'd heal up just fine.

"No, they died." She sucked in a huge breath. "Thing is, while a lot of the evil has disappeared, I still feel some left. Someone got away."

Mara looked me in the eye and a shiver ran down my spine. "Not Quincy. He was the first one I set on fire. Before I brought the building down, he had burnt to a crisp."

Something did feel off though. In addition to the normal scents surrounding a fire, I smelled something else, too. I looked around, and while there was no one anywhere near us, the hair on the back of my neck stood on end, and I felt like I was being watched.

After doing a three-sixty spin, I took off walking away from the fire. The further I got, the more I smelled something familiar. It was light but I smelled sulfur and tasted metal. It wasn't my own personal scent either. Had another dragon been here?

"Mara, do you sense anyone else?" If there was

anyone else here, I knew the grand witch would know it.

Mara's wide eyes confirmed my own suspicions before her words did. "There was something, but it's not here anymore." She met my eyes. "I know it's not possible, but I think there was another dragon here."

"Do you think they had kidnapped another dragon just in case they couldn't kill me?" While I was really excited about their being another dragon, I really hoped they didn't have anyone else in their grasp. The other option, that one of my kind had turned evil, well, that was unthinkable, especially since, as far as I knew, he or she might be the only other dragon alive.

"It's very conceivable, but unlikely." Mara shook her head. "How he would have found another dragon is beyond me."

"We have to find her or him," I declared firmly. "Whoever they are must be a prisoner. We can't leave them to the Shadow Walkers." My family was dead, but if there were more dragons out there, I wanted to meet them more than almost anything. As I took a deep breath to try and calm myself, I knew I had to find out for sure, and what's more, I needed to save them.

Mara looked like she was going to say something else, but before she could, Vlad put his arm around my shoulder. "Don't worry, Alyson. We will find whoever it is and save them. But first, we have to head back to base."

"Actually, the very first thing you should do is to please take me back to my safe house." Mara smiled. "I need to get back to my coven and see how many survived. We will offer our healing services to any paranormal caught up in this battle for power. I imagine there will be quite a few injured out there."

"Right, let's see if our car survived the fire." Vlad led us back to the Mustang we'd driven up in. It was sitting there with soot on it, but otherwise it looked fine.

"Do you think we should try the phones, just to see if my hunch was accurate?" I asked after we dropped Mara off with her daughters and her coven.

Vlad arched an eyebrow as we headed to base. "What hunch?"

"I figured it was magic keeping the phones from working, especially since we had dial tones on landlines and could hear ringing on our cell but had no service bars. It just seemed very odd." I pulled out my phone but Vlad took it out my hands.

"No phone calls while driving. I'll call." Vlad opened my phone and dialed.

"Steve? The phones work again?" Vlad was smiling while he spoke with Steve, our section chief. After a few moments of back-and-forth conversation, Vlad held a hand over the speaker to catch me up.

"They had no problem taking back the base. I figured we could catch him up on what happened with our case when we get there. First, we need to figure out how exactly to explain you burning down Quincy and the Walkers with your dragon fire. While Steve knows, we need a cover story for the official public records."

"True." I thought for a moment. "Could we alter the story so it was Mara who fried everyone? She is the great witch and has the power to do it, right?" I hadn't actually seen her start any magical fires, but who knew with that woman?

"Not quite, but the FBI probably doesn't know exactly what she's capable of. I'll have to tell her our story so she can corroborate if she's ever asked." Vlad shrugged. "Besides, even if we make something up, the FBI will put their own non-paranormal spin on it."

"That's true, but let's go with Mara being the one to destroy the evil mage, anyway. It's a better story. What do you say we get a good night's sleep after we are done with everything back at base and then tomorrow meet up for a celebratory drink? I'm buying."

"I'll buy us dinner, then. I think we deserve a night on the town after this case." Vlad smiled.

"Really? You don't want to go visit your ladies? Get a top off on blood and some hanky panky?" That came out far snarkier than I intended.

I mean, I had never had a problem with Vlad fulfilling his needs in the past. His time, his life. Now, something inside of me rebelled at the idea of Vlad seeing other women. I certainly wasn't going to feed his appetite, but I didn't like the idea of him getting his needs met by some skank.

I probably just needed some sleep. We had spent an awful lot of time together the past few days. Some time away from him would do us both good.

"I don't need blood right now." He took a step toward me and offered me his hand. "I would much rather spend a night off work with you, Alyson."

My cheeks heated up as he spoke, and I prayed he couldn't see my blushing.

"Thanks, I think I would like it too." I bit my lip before I could say anything to cause me more embarrassment.

THANK YOU FOR READING!

Curious about what happens to Alyson & Vlad next?

Find out soon!

AUTHOR'S NOTE

Dear reader, if you REALLY want to read the next FBI Dragon novel- I've got a bit of bad news for you.

Unfortunately, **Amazon will not tell you when the next comes out.**

You'll probably never know about my next books, and you'll be left wondering what happened to Alyson and Vlad. That's rather terrible.

There is good news though! There are three ways you can find out when the next book is published:

1) You join my mailing list by clicking here.

2) You follow J.A. on his Facebook page or join his Facebook Group. Alternatively, you can like J.L.'s Facebook Page. We always announce my new

books in both those places as well as interact with fans.

3) You follow J.A. on Amazon. You can do this by going to the store page (or clicking this link) and clicking on the Follow button that is under the author picture on the left side.

If you follow J.A., Amazon will send you an email when he publishes a book. You'll just have to make sure you check the emails they send.

Doing any of these, or all three for best results, will ensure you find out about my next book when it is published.

If you don't, Amazon will never tell you about my next release. Please take a few seconds to do one of these so that you'll be able to join Alyson and Vlad on their next adventure.

A WORD FROM J.L.

Thank you all so much for picking up my latest book! I wrote this with J.A. Cipriano, it was my first time writing a full-length book with another author. I learned a lot from J.A. and I think this is my best book yet! I hope you enjoyed it.

While finishing this book I found out I had a rare heart condition and ended up in the hospital for open-heart surgery. All went very good. I'm healing faster than anyone thought, although, I am getting tired of laying around and watching T.V. I must give a huge shout-out to J.A. and thank him for finishing up all of the loose ends while I was in the hospital and then at home recovering. He has been great to work with. I hope you check out some of his other books as well as mine!

When I first started writing A Ritual of Fire I wasn't exactly sure where we were going with this story. We had an outline, but it was vague (on purpose). We spent several weeks going back and forth with the outline and the first 15K words trying to get it right. I knew something wasn't quite right, as did J.A., so he sent it to a developmental editor who put us back on track. We wrote out a great opening sequence, but when it came down to final edits that scene did nothing for moving the story forward. I have those original first few chapters and have loaded them up on my website as a special "Bonus" for all who read this far! Come on by and read the outtakes from A Ritual of Fire! https://jlhendricksauthor.com/free-short-stories/

I also want to thank everyone who helped make this a fantastic first book in my latest series! Our editors, cover designer, and even the ARC readers who got back to me with a few questions on where the story is going. By asking those questions, I know they are really invested in this new series!

When J.A. first approached me about writing a new series with him, I was completely shocked! He's such a great author and I really admired him and his writing. Of course I said yes right away! I think the story really took advantage of a woman/man writing team! We have two main characters; one is female and the other male. Having authors who represent both sexes really added to the characters' dimension and made them seem more real, even if they are paranormal creatures. LOL

I totally look forward to writing the next book with J.A. Cipriano! I hope you look forward to reading it!

-Jen